THE DEEP TRANSLUCENT POND

The Deep Translucent Pond

A novel
by

JAMES SHELLEY

Adelaide Books
New York / Lisbon
2021

THE DEEP TRANSLUCENT POND

A novel

By James Shelley

Published by Adelaide Books, New York / Lisbon
adelaidebooks.org

Editor-in-Chief
Stevan V. Nikolic

For any information, please address Adelaide Books
at info@adelaidebooks.org

or write to:

Adelaide Books
244 Fifth Ave. Suite D27
New York, NY, 10001

ISBN: 978-1-956635-79-9

Printed in the United States of America

Contents

Chapter 1

The Triangulum

Jerome Konigsberg had not walked in a multi-cultural neighborhood for years and never while wearing an Armani business suit. Successive storefront windows reflected three faceless young men in hoodies keeping pace with him on the other side of the street. He wondered if his Audi would still be at the meter when this meeting was over.

He entered the coffee shop on Coventry and snaked past glowing lap-tops and smart phones to a corner table—the same as two weeks ago—where a heavyset, goateed man was carefully writing on a yellow legal pad with an old-fashion fountain pen. Like their first meeting, he was unsure how to address him. *Mr. Magus?* During a rare appearance at a poetry reading that summer, Literary League president Phil Lundy had introduced this man to the audience as "The Black Magus", a nom de plume change from the 90s that remained cryptic. Especially since he didn't appear to be black.

"Good morning," Jerome said. The man known as the Black Magus continued to write. A short-sleeve working man's shirt gave him a proletariat look and Jerome regretted not leaving his suit jacket in the car. *If my car is stolen, at least I still have the Armani*. He draped it on the back of the wooden chair, plopped his i-phone on the table and extended his right hand. "Thank you for selecting me. It's an honor to be here."

"Put that away!" the Black Magus snarled, still writing. Jerome withdrew his hand. The Black Magus pointed at the phone. "*That*!" Jerome slipped it into his coat pocket. The Black Magus spread his fingers atop the yellow tablet. "I have completed the Prologue to the project the three of us will complete. Read it while we await your fellow pupil."

Jerome realized he lacked experience dealing with a 1970s nationally-known poet, in more recent decades Cleveland's most famous recluse. Phil Lundy's warning echoed: "He doesn't do well in public places." The Black Magus slid the pad—which displayed elegantly handwritten paragraphs—across the table to him. Jerome righted it and began reading.

Entrance Exam

Word circulated that the Black Magus would be taking on two new poetry fellows. Over a dozen poets interviewed with him individually for the highly coveted spots. After ten seconds of polite small talk to begin each interview, he handed each interviewee a slip of paper on which was written one question: Have you ever seen a cloud move?

Some of the applicants harrumphed. Others angled their heads, trying to conjure a cloud moving. Those who did not answer within five seconds were disqualified.

Four applicants out of nine advanced. The first was a young nurse, Natalija. After reading the question she immediately looked up: "I've actually seen two clouds moving in opposite directions."

The second was an attorney named Jerome. After reading the question he replied: "Two weeks ago—no three—I watched a cloud move across a full moon. Almost a full moon."

Asked to submit sample poems, the submissions of two other applicants were deemed over-machined. The nurse and the lawyer submitted verses acceptably un-machined. They were selected.

The orientation meeting of The Tenth Triangulum took place in the Arabica Coffee House on September 8th at 10am.

Jerome glanced at his watch. It was 10:01am. He liked the name Natalija and wondered what she looked like. He kept two fingers on the pad to stave the other man's reach. "Your… Prologue is certainly up to the minute." He remembered being interviewed and how he had been on the verge of "harrumphing". Instead—as if it was a job interview—he said what he knew the interviewer wanted to hear. Afterwards he wondered why he chose a nocturnal image for his fabrication.

Jerome re-scanned the writing. He wanted to know what "over-machined" meant but his lawyer's eye circled back to another term. "The Tenth Triangulum. I am unfamiliar with that term. How is it relevant to my poetry fellowship?"

The Black Magus looked up, but not at him. A slender young woman with reddish-blonde hair in a loose bun deftly slipped into the chair next to Jerome's.

"Sorry, I think I'm late."

Jerome, immediately noticing a prettiness, smiled. "I'm Jerome."

She nervously shook his hand. "Natalija."

"I'm getting a coffee, Natalija. What can I get you?"

Before she could answer the Black Magus cleared his throat and read aloud from his note pad. "Jerome Konigsberg?"

Jerome half-raised his right hand. "Here?

"Jewish?"

"On my father's side."

"Your mother's faith?"

Jerome twisted his lips. "None of the above."

"Natalija Gasper?"

The young woman waved. "Here."

"Catholic?"

Although not wearing a crucifix, she touched the base of her neck. "How is it I look Catholic?"

"Your hands."

"I have Catholic hands?"

"Look at any Raphael Madonna and you will see your hands. No one painted a young mother's hands more beautifully than Raphael."

"I'm not a mother."

"If I had a fever, I would want a hand like yours caressing my forehead." Natalija withdrew her hands from the tabletop. The Black Magus switched back to Jerome, narrowing his eyes. "Because your parents were at odds, I'm guessing you lack exposure to formal religion."

"Is that a requirement?"

"No. But *this* is." From a large brown envelope, he pulled out a color print of DaVinci's Last Supper, one edge jagged as if torn from a book. He pointed to Christ in the center.

Jerome stared at the iconic image of Jesus, then pushed his chair back from the table. "I was under the impression this would go in a different direction." He reached behind for his suit jacket.

The Black Magus tapped on Christ. "Before you flee, please answer this. We know who he is. But what do you see?"

Jerome and Natialija leaned closer. The Black Magus traced a finger around the image.

"A triangle?" Natalija chimed. The outline of the seated Christ, framed by the window, formed a perfect triangle with rounded corners.

"The triangle is the most stable shape," the Black Magus said. "Or in its three-dimensional form, a pyramid. It cannot be pushed over. Cheops knew this. DaVinci too." He rested his hands on the picture. "Over the next ten weeks, the three of us will form an equilateral triangle. You two will each compose a side, and myself the base. If we can stay intact, no one can push over our transformation."

Natalija nodded enthusiastically, slightly rocking. Jerome wondered whether she was being polite, or diffident. "I'm not quite getting the triangle thing," Jerome said. "And what kind of transformation are we talking about?"

The Black Magus opened his hands. "We will let the softer sediment wash away and see what remains."

"That certainly explains it," Jerome quipped. He turned to Natalija to subtly raise an eyebrow; she was gazing at a far corner of the table, window light catching her eyes, a striking green. The Black Magus continued. "Each week you will bring a new poem. Since I find the term "poem" limiting, please substitute "writing" for "poem". Each writing must be handwritten to avoid over-machining. Every week's writing will be based on one of the Ten Books."

Jerome bent two fingers into his cheekbone. "The fellowship application never mentioned anything like that, only that the poems resulting from this—excuse me, the writings—would be added to the writings of the previous fellows and published together. What are these ten books?"

The Black Magus handed them each a white envelope. "Review the contents between now and our first session next week."

"A syllabus?" Jerome smirked.

"If that's what you want it to be."

"I've never been published," Natalija said, the finely-tapered fingers of one hand fanned across her chin. "Thank you for picking me." Jerome, a modestly published poet, was relieved to hear of his fellow pupil's inexperience.

The Black Magus closed his eyes and opened his hands. "Whatever you bring to The Tenth Triangulum, it must have a birth-edge. No shrink-wrapped words. I want to see blood from the midwife's hands on your aprons." He opened his eyes and put the picture back into the large envelope. "Questions?"

Before they could respond he signaled to someone. A short man with long grey hair flowing from under a Cleveland Indians hat bounced over to the table. "I'm Tony," he smiled, "The chauffeur." He warmly shook their hands.

The Black Magus pushed down on a cane to rise from the table. "Next week we discuss the entry writings which led to your selection. We meet at my residence."

Outside the coffee shop, Jerome and Natalija watched the twosome walk away, the larger man trundling with a cane and the other loping at his side like a silver-haired teenager.

"A bit of an odd couple." Jerome observed.

"Kinda cute," Natalija shrugged. Jerome had been trying to place her accent, so slight he wondered if it was affected. In full daylight he was again struck by her green eyes. She matched him in height and he straightened to nudge his 5'8" higher than hers.

"So what do you think?" Jerome asked.

"He was uptight."

"I've heard he doesn't get out much."

Natalija shielded her eyes from the sun. "What interested you in this?"

"He was still pretty well-known when I started writing poetry in college. I didn't know about the fellowship until recently. I applied because.....I'm looking for something different. And you?"

Her eyes fluttered. "Same as you. I'm searching for a way." Jerome started to protest that he hadn't said that, but she was already moving away. She half-waved. "Have to get to work."

Stooped shoulders and her bunned hair made her look older from behind, despite an attractive slenderness. He was intrigued enough by her manner and looks to prolong the encounter. "You're a nurse?"

"An LPN," she replied over her shoulder.

"See you next week." He watched her hurry away, regretting he had lied and wouldn't be seeing her next week, nor likely ever again.

Relieved to see his moonlight-blue Audi still at the meter, Jerome got in, flicked the envelope onto the passenger seat and scrolled his contacts for Phil Lundy. If he was to give back his fellowship, best to do so now. About to call Phil, he set down the phone and opened the envelope. Inside were two sheets, the second a hand drawn map to the Black Magus' house in Eastlake. The first sheet displayed the same elegant penmanship as the Black Magus' Prologue:

The Ten Books of The Triangulum Project.

I. The Book of What is Missed
II. The Book of What is Sacred
III. The Book of Slow Leaks
IV. The Book of Lightness
V. The Book of Waking Up

VI. The Book of Hypermodernity
VII. The Book of Insecurities
VIII. The Book of Leaps
IX. The Book of Reconnecting
X. The Clearing

The topics looked interesting. But why present this information in a sealed envelope when it could have been presented for discussion at the coffee shop? Like a normal person would have done? Along the bottom edge was a line in smaller handwriting. He raised it next to the window to decipher: *Make the Leap. Love. Surrender.*

Jerome sucked in his lips and set down the letter. He lifted a finger to tap Phil's number then yanked back his hand. He gazed out the windshield through his ghostly reflection. Finding a way out was worth one more desperate lunge.

Chapter 2

The Hole

The Window Chair

The Black Magus ambled into what had once been his father's bedroom and set a cup of instant coffee on the small table next to a sturdy wooden chair. The chair was turned—as it had been since his father's death fifteen years ago—to face out an uncurtained first-floor window. After sitting, he closed his eyes to better feel the yellow September sunlight penetrate pleasingly across his large body. *My chest still rises and falls. Thank you!*

Sporting smooth arm rests, the chair remained surprisingly solid, though over the years he had successively flattened several portable seat pads. Two wooden bookcases, each shelf neatly rowed with softcover books, stood against one wall. A six-foot long folding table, ten manilla folders evenly spaced across it's top, was centered against the opposite wall. He sometimes regretted expunging his father's bedroom furniture, but rationalized that the oldest piece, the chair, not only symbolically remained, but had taken on a special role.

The view through the window of an overgrown field beyond his small backyard permitted him to keep his worldview seasonally analog, trading snow eddies in January for pollen smoke gusting through new grasses in June. Tony, when he peeked into the room during visits, often joked he could tell which month it was by the chair's position. Years of lateral travel in front of the window had etched striations into the worn wood floor. As the sun migrated south, the Black Magus incrementally "grunted" the chair to the left until reversing directions on December 21, allowing himself to keep up with Sol's bathing light as the seasons changed. Twice a year the chair occupied a point dead center: March 21 and September 21.

He started to unbutton his shirt to expose a patch of psoriasis to the healing sunlight but, remembering that he would have guests this morning, he smoothed the front of his blue shirt instead. For one last time, Phil Lundy was delivering to him the gift of two new pupils.

A continuing force on the Literary League board, Phil had fought yearly battles to keep the Project's two annual fellowships and $1500 teaching stipend funded. His argument was the same every year: *"Cleveland's greatest poet since Hart Crane is on disability, living in near poverty and—if we fail to renew this—will languish as an under-utilized cultural resource"*.

When Phil first bragged of his well-crafted appeal's positive impact on the board, the Black Magus' response was ambiguously appreciative: "Under-utilized? One must never be that."

But this year, younger board members had prevailed, and the fellowship funds were to be re-routed into grants to send young inner-city poets to a national conference. Phil broke the news to him the previous week: after nine years of tutoring two aspiring poets each Fall, this year—the tenth—would be the last. The Black Magus would have to surrender his pupils' accumulated poems—spawned under this tutelage—to the fellowship project's culmination: a published chapbook series. "It's just as well," Phil added. "Those early pupils of yours have been waiting all these years to see their stuff in print."

The Black Magus nodded silently. *They know how to be patient. They have been to The Clearing.*

His hand slightly trembling, he sipped some coffee then rested the warm mug atop his right thigh. He thought about his new pupils. He liked that the young woman was 30 and the man 40. Their combined ages, versus his, achieved symmetry. He also liked their opposite qualities which had seeped through in their entrance interviews and entry writings.

The man, despite career success as an attorney at Squires Sanders, was at risk of *un-becoming*. His rowboat was slowly sinking yet he was unable to either row for shore, or bail. Perhaps he was intrigued with the sharpening thoughts which accompanied sinking. Or maybe he was tired of living.

Conversely, the woman was trying *to become*. Entangled in seaweed on a cold pebbly beach, she was clawing nakedly toward a place to rest, and then stand. A quiet fierceness to do so—along with her copper hair and slight accent, which reminded him of his first case worker, an attractive Turkish woman—intrigued him. What he could not ascertain was the depth of her wound. If too deep, he might not be able to save her.

Despite different pain, both pupils were reaching for something they wanted desperately to touch. If he guided their hands, perhaps they could do something for him in return. He too was trying to touch something. He thought of the picture hanging in the bathroom—hand-drawn in colored pencil—of the small pond in a wooded clearing radiating submerged light. A week never passed when he didn't find an area to touch up, adding a fleck of blue or dot of yellow, then standing back to see if the mysterious pond-light revealed anything new. Only one thing seemed certain: its light came from a deep place. He glazed into a stare and sadly smiled. “Maybe this time, we new three will have a reach long enough”. A voice in his head flashed caution. *If.....they come.*

The Practice Meeting

Jerome turned onto a residential street with no sidewalks. He slowly passed modest 1950s bungalows and shoebox-shaped ranch homes situated on relatively spacious lots. It still felt like a mistake—abandoning conventional therapies to address his “disorder”, the only shared terminology in differing pronouncements from three psychiatrists. But he had left himself an “out”. If he had trouble finding the house, or didn’t like the look of it, he would turn around.

The Black Magus’ roadside mailbox was numberless, but by interpolating addresses on neighboring mailboxes Jerome guessed which driveway. A ragged line of trees and shrubby growth obscured the house. He drove down a worn gravel drive which straddled a ridge of grass, splashing through puddles which, after several dry days, struck him as anomalies. A white cottage-like house that looked like it should be on a lake emerged. He pulled onto an area of flattened grass and left the car running. White paint flakes encircling the house’s foundation faintly glowed like a derelict aura. There were no other cars.

“This is too weird.” As he reached to put his car in reverse, an older model Corolla parked alongside from which Natalija quickly emerged. She jerked her head and long red-blond hair, un-bunned this time, flashed behind her. Jerome immediately turned his car off and got out.

“Good Morning,” he called over.

Natalija stopped and turned. "Oh. I thought I might be late. Maybe not." They came together and studied the small one-story home. "Are those tiny trees growing in the gutter?" Natalija asked. Across the front gutter, maple seedlings had sprouted like small pennants.

"They'll be changing color in another month," Jerome replied. "I'm sure it will look quite festive."

Natalija's eyes fluttered as she lowered her gaze to the front door. "We better not be tardy for our first class."

They climbed moss-tinged stone steps to the front door. Several coats of paint obliterated the doorbell. Jerome slipped an arm through a tear in the screen door and knocked.

"Enter!" a voice bellowed from the other side.

They entered a tiny vestibule which opened to a small living room and a faint smell of cigarettes and vending machine coffee. The Black Magus sat in a worn leather armchair wearing the same neatly pressed light blue button-down work shirt. He spread his arms.

"Welcome to the Tenth Triangulum!" He pointed to two wooden chairs with upholstered seats, commandeered from an adjoining dining room. The three chairs, positioned about five feet apart and angled toward the center, formed equi-distant points of a triangle. Other than a folding tray stand next to the Black Magus' chair and a floor lamp in a corner, the room was barren of furniture, but clean. A small fan in a corner quietly hummed.

Sidestepping threadbare areas of the carpet, Natalija walked to the chair to the left and Jerome to the other. About to sit, the Black Magus pointed, crisscrossing his arms. "Please switch." They complied, Jerome moving to the Black Magus' left. Although it was warm, Jerome did not remove his suit jacket. Natalija, in jeans and a long blue sweater, remained perched on the edge of her chair.

"Instant coffee?" the Black Magus proffered.

"No thank you," they simultaneously replied.

Jerome opened the flap on his leather document holder and withdrew the fellowship guidelines, printed from the Literary League's website. "Question. Last week you referred to this as a 'Triangulum' and you said it again just now. The Literary League's website never describes such a thing."

The Black Magus brought his hands together. "The Triangulum Project is my appellation. This will be its tenth constellation. Thus, The Tenth Triangulum."

Natalija tilted forward. "And why do you call it that?"

The large man gazed between them, his nostrils expanding and contracting. "The Triangulum Galaxy is the most distant light we can see with the naked eye. It contains a nebula, NGC 604. Radiation from new stars blows holes in the nebula providing a view into its black interior—a star birthing factory." He opened his hands. "The Tenth Triangulum's first order of business is to understand holes." He opened a folder and handed each of them a single sheet of hand-copied verses written in the same calligraphic penmanship Jerome had admired at the coffee shop. "I ask that you read silently."

The Hole

During a marathon
A black hole chases each runner
Those who complete the race
Proclaim themselves "hole-beaters"

Later that week at breakfast
The hole-beaters notice a place is set for the hole
And hastily lace up their running shoes

But you
Can see through the breakneck absurdity
Of striving to be a fast-moving surface speck
Unable to act, rest both hands
On the bulging emptiness within

Do not let your hole become too precious!
Fill it as needed
Leaving just enough room to
Still reach into
The other world below

Bring back quiet secrets
To the frantic ones above

The Black Magus drummed fingers on the chair arms. "We, in The Triangulum, do not run from holes. Neither do we indulge them. We are charged with bringing back quiet secrets."

Jerome gripped his jaw. "Who is charging us to do this?"

"No one. And everyone. Me. You." He pointed at Natalija. "Her."

They both looked at Natalija, her blue-jeaned knees forming a table for her folder. She raised a fist. "I'm all in!" An awkward silence nudged her to continue. "So....each week we bring a new poem?"

"A new writing," the Black Magus corrected. "At the end of each session, you can make one alteration to what you bring before submitting—a line, a word, a comma. Or nothing. It is important the secrets you bring remain intact."

Jerome bit his lower lip, wishing he could record this. The Black Magus resumed. "We will follow the order of the ten books from the list I gave you at the coffee shop. Next week you will bring three un-machined, hand-written copies of a writing for the *Book of What is Missed."* Jerome opened his mouth to ask a question, but the Black Magus pressed on. "Today, we discuss your entry writings which helped you earn the fellowship." He turned to Jerome. "We begin with yours." He handed a copy to each of them.

"Should I read aloud?" Jerome asked.

"I can tell more from your handwriting than from a playback voice." They each quietly read Jerome's writing.

The Regaining

I am realistic enough to know
If I stumble upon The Grail
It won't be a chalice, haloed in
radial spokes of blinding white

I only hope
like the sighting of a rare bird
I recognize it before it slips away
long enough
to help keep my head above water

Scanning the horizon for rescue:
the next shimmer of light

After a few minutes the Black Magus removed his glasses and held them out toward Jerome. "During the next ten weeks, over the crest of waves, you will indeed see shimmers. But there will also be cold depths. There is life there too. I would be remiss as a rabbi if I did not take you there."

Jerome's brows went up. "You're a rabbi?"

"Rabbi means teacher."

"Is that what we should call you?"

"My pupils have never called me anything. Which could mean I am many things."

Natalija leaned forward onto her crossed legs. "Its awkward... not knowing how to address you." She had a pleasing way, Jerome noticed, of holding up her right hand when speaking, aesthetically upturning her wrist and unfurling slender fingers.

The Black Magus replaced his glasses and, ignoring Natalija's comment, handed each of them a copy of her entry writing. "Read silently."

The Door

Alone on a cold December sidewalk
a door opens a few feet behind me
I hear it as a soft whooshing—the vacuum seal
to a hidden place is broken

I turn around

Botticelli's goddess of Spring, red-blonde
tresses lifting and tangling,
steps through a rectangular pane of light.
Chastely dressed in a floral-patterned gown
she coyly tilts her head
holds out a shimmering cup.

I open a hand to accept, then hesitate.
Is this the way out? The way in?
Or is this what death is like?
Did I in fact
just die?

The blossom-scented breeze reverses
warm light retracts
the door is closing
I pull back fingers just in time

As the door vacuums shut,
I smile.

For a moment, at least
A door was opened
To me!

Jerome was relieved to note a lack of technical finesse. He especially didn't like the exclamation point at the end, like the forced semi-colon smiles at the end of so many of his female co-workers' emails. At the same time her writing was intriguingly both heavy *and* light. Less dense than his poems which, he felt, often struggled for ground clearance.

The Black Magus contemplated Natalija. *She knows who Botticelli is.* "Why are you frowning?"

Natalija's tried to smile. "I've never been to a poetry workshop. To be honest, I don't even read poetry. At least by people still alive. I just write."

The large man in the short-sleeved proletariat shirt pointed behind her. "What is over there?"

Natalija turned. "Your front door?"

"Did it almost close on your fingers?"

"No."

"And it never will. I am not as beautiful as your goddess of Spring. But the cup I hold out is just as full."

Natalija smiled and turned her head cutely. "I thank you for that."

Jerome chortled. The Black Magus made notes on a yellow legal pad. Without looking up he tilted his pen at Jerome. "You used the word 'shimmer', and you…" he pointed at Natalija, "used 'shimmering'. You are both searching for the same light."

Jerome, who had been eyeing his watch, suddenly felt a strange backward-forward jostle, a physical sensation he remembered as a student travelling in Europe: a train engine coupling with passenger cars.

At 10:50 am, after more discussion on his pupils' writings, the Black Magus announced that—in order to simulate the next ten weeks—they could make one alteration to their entry writings before re-submitting. At 10:59 he closed the session by saying he would see them next week for *The Book of What is Missed.*

"Can you….elaborate on that?" Jerome asked.

"If," the Black Magus replied, "you were to contribute something of 60 words or less to an anthology called *The Book of What is Missed,* what would it be?"

Jerome slowly nodded. "O—kay." He stood up and Natalija followed suit. As they reached the front door the Black Magus called after them.

"Do not ask me any questions about those who have come before you. As far as you are concerned, you are the first."

"Wouldn't think of it," Jerome replied.

They exited and he watched them through a window walk to their cars where they paused to converse. *The lawyer is trying to decide if he is attracted to her. Perhaps that is what will bring him back.* He hoped so. The Tenth Triangulum showed unusual promise. "Yes", yes," he said aloud to the two empty chairs. "I think we will constellate well."

Outside, Natalija scanned the peeling house paint and moss mottled roof. "Should we offer to help with this?"

Jerome surveyed the lawn, probably uncut for several weeks. "He might like it this way: Un-machined."

The late morning sun glared through a thin cloud layer making Natalija's eyes more gray than green. Jerome wanted to say two things to her and led with the easier one.

"You have a slight accent."

"My parents are from Slovenia."

He nodded, unsure whether to ask about Slovenia or say the second thing. Before he could act she half-waved. "See you next week.....fellow pupil." She perused his Audi. "Pretty."

Pulling onto the road, Jerome punched the gas and squeezed the wheel, regretting not saying the second thing. To see how it would have sounded, he spoke it now. "He said we're both searching for the same light. Pretty cool. Don't you think?"

Chapter 3

The Book of What is Missed

The Quarry

The Black Magus, seated in his outward facing window chair, sipped instant coffee in morning sunlight. He was grateful the night had passed surprisingly well. The Night Daemon had not disturbed him.

Once or twice a week while sleeping, he experienced trouble breathing and awakened to feel the Night Daemon sitting cross-legged on his chest. He would swat hard at the invisible weight and, a few seconds later, hear his uninvited guest hit the floor. In the old days the Daemon would then go fuss his dog Nestor. When Nestor convulsed and whimpered he knew his poor dog was dreaming a wolf.

Savoring the rare feeling of a good night's rest, he allowed the field's golden rod and dewy morning sparkles to ease him into the day. A dead blue jay several feet from the window marred the attempt. It was beautiful—hues of blue only seen in perfect stillness. But its inertness unsettled him. He wished he handled dead things better. Perhaps if he had served in a war like his father. His closest encounter with death was almost comedic by comparison. But it had given him a place to return to.

Always, when he remembered, he heard Tony's frantic, 18-year old voice cry out: *Don't let go!*

They learned about the quarry from Lundy's older sister, a student at Oberlin. He, Lundy, Shome, and Tony made the one hour trip in Tony's '62 Ford Fairlane. Shome brought along a special treat—sinsemilla buds ornamented with tiny droplets of THC, like a tiny Christmas tree.

They parked on the side of a shady rural road and, lugging towels and a 12-pak of Strohs, started up a narrow trail into woods. After ten minutes they came to a long-abandoned stone quarry, its black-streaked sides dropping precipitously to a large pool of opaque emerald water.

Lundy, who liked to talk in extremes, didn't disappoint them. "My sister says no one has ever seen the bottom. Not even scuba divers."

The tangy pine-scented weed sucked in like a mentholated cigarette. Suitably buzzed, they eyed a thick hemp rope dangling from a branch jutting over the cliff. Tony, ever the bold one, used a nearby stick to pull the rope closer. They gathered at the edge and looked down. Directly below, tumbled rocks formed a steep staircase up from the water to the cliff edge.

"Don't let go until you clear those bad boys," Tony said. Gripping the rope, he back-pedaled, let out a rebel yell and charged off the edge. At the furthest point of his swing he let go, seconds later shattering the placid surface. Surfacing, he jerked his head, whipping back his long wet hair. "Dudes! You gotta do it!"

Shome secured the rope on its backswing and went next. Much bigger than Tony, his splash jarred the hermetic stillness. Lundy stepped up next. The least coordinated, he hit the water at a funny angle. The others howled. Lundy climbed up the tumbled rocks to the cliff edge and—at the sight of his bright red skin—they howled again.

Heartened that he couldn't do worse, he took the rope. Tony came alongside and, peering through stringy wet hair, whispered. "Don't let go until you're way out there. Do you want me to yell when?" He shook his head hoping the others hadn't heard and backpedaled to get a running start.

"Put the hoover on shag, Bear!" Lundy shouted.

Gripping the rope, he ran off the cliff edge. At the furthest point of his arc he let go, dropping 30 feet into the emerald pool. Surfacing, he triumphantly yelped. Although the water was pleasant at the surface, it froze his ankles and he quickly swam for the tumbled rock stair case.

After a few more swings apiece they smoked another sumptuous, Shome-rolled joint then stretched out on the warm rock shelf to bake dry. "We're lying on stone...stoned," someone muttered.

A while later he sat up, unsure how much time had passed. Everything around him had a three-dimensional, hyper-quality—the trees, the clouds, the smaller rocks, the rope's hemp fibers. They had forgotten to secure the rope and it dangled three or four feet from the edge, seemingly suspended over nothingness.

He stood up, damp hair coldly tickling his hot shoulders. He walked to the cliff moving stiffly in his damp cut-offs and used the stick to retrieve the rope. His friends were still stretched out, arms or T-Shirts draped over eyes. It was time to roust them from their stupor. He backed up, counted quietly to three, then charged off the cliff.

He swung out beyond the tumbled rocks. About to let go, he glanced at the spot below where he would land and saw a dark shape rising toward the water surface. He held on, swinging back to the cliff edge. Unable to spin around to get a foothold, he swung back over the water. The dark shape was gone, but he still wouldn't let go. When he swung back the other way he was short of the cliff. Swinging in smaller arcs, the rope came to rest four feet from the cliff edge, about twenty feet above the jumbled rocks. "Help!" he cried. "HELP"

His friends wobbled upright. Tony was the first to snap out it. "DON'T LET GO!" He scrambled to the edge and extended the stick. "Grab it!"

"I gotta hold the rope with both hands!"

Tony ran into the woods and sprinted back holding a thick prong-ended stick. He pushed it against the rope higher up. "We gotta push him past the rocks! Come on you assholes!"

Shome and Lundy grabbed hold of the stick behind him and together they pushed. After moving the rope a few feet Shome grunted, "Just like the marines at Iwo Jima." Lundy collapsed in laughter. Then Shome started laughing and fell away. Then *he* started laughing. His grip loosened. He was going to fall onto pointy rocks yet couldn't stop laughing.

Tony unleashed a guttural scream and, gripping the stick like a lance, charged forward. To nudge the rope past the rocks he extended himself over the edge, the pushback from the rope barely preventing him from going over. Shome and Lundy, no longer laughing, hooked fingers through his belt loops. "LET GO!" Tony yelled. "NOW!"

Because it came from Tony, he knew he wouldn't die. When he opened his eyes underwater, the mossy side of a boulder was inches from his face.

Remembering that moment, the Black Magus gripped his face to suppress a shudder. He sipped coffee and went to where the re-play always took him: the dark shape in the water. Was it a cloud shadow? Had he magnified a fish? Or did the quarry's unknown depths harbor something else? What if he had let go, plunged into the water, and nothing had happened? Would his life have been different?

He gazed at the lifeless blue jay, then abruptly set down his coffee and tilted his head back. "And so, you old fool, you chose to live your life metaphysically rather than physically." It seemed a fair sentencing for his cowardice: To each day swing out over an imaginal world, let go, and swim with the dark shapes.

The morning sun through the window had drifted below his chest, resting warmly atop his lap. His two pupils would arrive in a few hours for the *Book of What is Missed* and he needed to prepare. He perused the utility table against the wall to the right. Across it were ten equally spaced folders, one for each year of the Triangulum Project. The tenth folder, empty, would begin today. He twisted his mouth, hoping the order of the ten topics—the same within each Triangulum folder—was finally set.

Originally, he had not even referred to the ten topics as Books, preferring "Distillates" as a more accurate term. He was confident he had identified ten pinnacles of hard substance that remained standing after years of hosing away softer sediment. But "Distillates" seemed too clinical and he switched to the more biblical sounding "Books". At one point he thought about expanding to 12 Books, arguably a more sacred number. But it made him think of a candelabrum with 12 candlesticks compared to one with ten. A ten-candlestick candelabrum seemed aesthetically trimmer, easier to raise with one arm.

He groaned out of the chair and ambled to the utility table. He straightened the first folder, labelled The First Triangulum, which contained the writings of his first two pupils, ten from each, one for each of the Ten Books. Moving down the line of folders he straightened and re-aligned them. When he got to the tenth folder, labelled The Tenth Triangulum, he opened it. It already contained ten writings, his own, one for each Book.

His contributed writings, carried through the previous nine Triangulum's, had transmuted within the dynamic of each new threesome. During the next ten weeks they would undergo more change, sometimes just a word or, in extreme cases, replacement with something altogether new. More importantly, ten weeks from now the folder would also contain the contributed writings from his two new pupils. He closed the folder, rested his hand upon it and whispered a prayer.

First Official Meeting of the 10th Triangulum

Natalija paused at the end of the driveway. Through the trees and tangled growth she spied Jerome's blue Audi. Last week's trepidation should have abated. Her entry writing had been well received and the Black Magus' kind words at the end of the session still echoed. *My front door will never close on your fingers.*

But the writing she brought today, to their first official meeting, was a piece of herself from a deeper excavation. She gazed down the driveway as if peering through a chain link fence. She put the gear shift in reverse. "No!" she yelled. "No more backpedalling!" She jammed the shift forward and splashed down the drive.

Jerome, arriving a few minutes earlier, had waited for Natalija and, with no sign of her Corolla, entered the house at 9:59am and took his designated seat in the triangular seating arrangement. The Black Magus, breathing loudly through his nose, didn't look up from the papers he perused. Jerome cleared his throat and looked around the room.

"How long have you lived here?"

"Twenty-six years."

"Which of your three poetry volumes from the 70s is your favorite?

"My published writings are in the past."

"So, Tony is your transportation?"

"Yes."

"Does he live close?"

"Not far."

Jerome, seeing his small talk volley categorically batted down, paused before asking the next question. "What was d.a. levy like?"

The Black Magus flinched, grunted, then nervously re-examined his yellow pad. Jerome thought it odd he had nothing to say about Cleveland's other famous poet from the 60s, their names commonly rolled into the same sentence, like Byron and Shelley. *Is he still affected by d.a.'s suicide after so many decades?*

Jerome reflexively patted his pockets for his cell phone even though he knew he had, for fear of a dirty look, left it in his car. He eyed the Black Magus who was scowling at his notes. *The rabbi can't function unless we are three.* What if Natalija didn't show? Would the session be cancelled? The Black Magus suddenly lifted his head like a dog catching a scent. Car tires crackled on the gravel drive. The triangle would be complete.

Natalija knocked then entered, wearing the same worn jeans and a long white sweater. Her hair, Jerome noted, displayed a new look: stringy and thin, the amber sheen gone. She sat, dropped some papers, picked them up, then hooked her thin hair behind her ears. "I am here. Present."

The Black Magus pressed his fingertips together. "Today we will explore what is missed. It could be anything. An object. A feeling. A person. Or maybe something from before our time".

"Anybody miss dinosaurs?" Jerome quipped. The Black Magus didn't smile. Natalija bent her head to her binder as if praying. Jerome noticed one of her socks was blue and the other striped.

"Since this is the first book," the Black Magus continued, "I will go first. What I bring to the *Book of What is Missed."* He handed each of them a copy of his writing.

No Moss Covered Trees

We, the largest generation
Sheer volume cutting new channels

In 1969 on a New York farm
We proclaimed ourselves the First People
No longer needing Elders, we pushed
Them into ravines
Until level with the surface

To replace such a loss
We elevated our children
We needed someone to follow

Now in our seventies
We should be dwelling in a noble forest:
Bearded, pipe-smoking men
And vigorous white-haired women
Resting against the massive roots
        of moss-covered trees

Instead,
We jog through mulched-over landscapes
Oldening bones faking youthful maneuvers

The New will always be superior to the Old
Even if it means dying
        in a shade less land

Following the Black Magus' lead, they re-read it, this time making notes. Natalija abruptly unbent her head and addressed the Black Magus. "How is it you still smolder?"

"Define smolder."

She extended a hand, expressively turning her palm upward. They waited, but nothing came out of her mouth.

The Black Magus sipped coffee. "Instead of gainful employment, I lifted rocks to seek oracles from blind salamanders."

Natalija closed the fingers of her uplifted hand, then elegantly unfurled them. "Why? To be different?"

The Black Magus opened his mouth to speak then averted his eyes. Jerome, surprised at his fellow pupil's sudden directness, moved fast to redirect the tension.

"The New York farm you reference—Woodstock obviously. Were you there?"

The Black Magus glared. "What, with those fools?" He fussed the papers in his lap. Natalija retracted her hand, crossed her arms, and re-bent her head. After an awkward silence the Black Magus turned to Jerome. "What do you bring to *The Book of What is Missed?*"

Jerome handed out his writing.

How?

The young man stands alone,
staring down

He cannot express it
but if he could, he might say:

"How is it I was delivered into cradling arms
and now the swaddling clothes
lie steaming at my feet?"

For a moment the young man looks up

The men who would show him what to do next
Are nowhere to be seen

Natalija abruptly turned to him. "Why does the young man say? Why doesn't he cry? Can you cry?" Her chin jutted with each phrase. Jerome realized he was getting the same blunt blows as the Black Magus. The Black Magus interceded.

"During the Great Depression, men wearing suits and fedora hats lined up for soup. Now, young men stand alone and silent, collapsed diapers warming the tops of their feet." Jerome wasn't sure if the Black Magus was implying that he had created a contemporary image equal in power to Depression era soup line photos; or if he was advising him to add more sensory information. Twisting his mouth, he jotted on his pad: *moist diaper warming tops of feet.*

The Black Magus launched into a discussion of tribal rites of passage and how they had disappeared for both males and females. Jerome, pleased he had struck a conversant chord, earnestly nodded. Natalija crossed and re-crossed her legs until forced to ask the Black Magus a question she had been dreading.

"Where is your bathroom?"

"Down the hall, first room on the left."

She went down a short, poorly lit hallway, the floor creaking under a thin carpet, and reached into a darkened room for a light switch. Chrome ensconced florescent lights buzzed to life on either side of a vanity mirror. Aware of her host's aversion to modernity she half-feared finding a bucket in lieu of a toilet. Instead, the lights revealed a small tidy bathroom with powder blue 1950s-porcelain fixtures. A flower-patterned shower curtain veiled the tub and a clean hand towel neatly draped a rack. The blue porcelain sparkled and there was a whiff of perfumed soap. Except for crumbling tile grout it could have been her grandmother's bathroom.

While seated, she noticed a small framed picture on the wall next to the door. After washing she approached it. Thick trunked trees overarched a small circular pond, a strange light radiating from under its surface. Emerging from woods in tattered clothes, a bearded, long-haired figure, eyes crazily enlarged and swollen tongue protruding from a gaping mouth, staggered toward the pond, his hands opening to the submerged light. In the upper right of the picture was calligraphic verse:

> *Finally, at twilight, beneath old trees:*
> *The Deep Translucent Pond....*

The picture was expertly drafted in colored pencil, although so over-laid with markings its surface shimmered. Tiny tears in the paper showed where repeated penciling had worn through. By contrast, the half-naked figure, slashed in simple black lines, appeared unmodified. The style reminded her of something from one of her British Lit courses. She tapped the picture frame until the name came. "William Blake!" she said aloud, remembering how the 18th century visionary mystic was both poet and painter. In the lower right she made out two letters, BM. She pressed her fingers to her chin, switched off the light, and re-entered the hallway.

The two men, who had been talking avidly when she left, silently perused their notes. She blushed, wondering if they had heard any noises from the bathroom. Back in her seat, the Black Magus turned to her. "And what do you bring to the *Book of What is Missed*?"

She started to hand out her writing, then hesitated. "I'm not sure I should share this."

The Black Magus pointed behind her. "That door will never close on your fingers."

She weakly smiled and handed out her writing.

Missing Melancholy

The periodic detour

trudging through shade so deep
not even ferns will grow

But there was always this:
The ability to keep walking
–even if just a shamble
to feel for, and move towards
the faintest movement of air

Depression has no such romance:
The fingertip groping for the outline of a door
Instead, finding the chute
where medication dispenses

Cordoning deep shade from
daily paths leaves two extremes:
A darkening room without a door,
or light we are afraid to turn off

And so, we choose–
Eyelids grotesquely pinned open
to the noonday sun

Jerome peeked at his two companions. The Black Magus had closed his eyes. Natalija stared at a point on the carpet. He felt that if he touched his pen to her shoulder she would shatter. He leaned sideways to penetrate her trance. "Very good," he whispered.

The Black Magus opened his eyes. He sipped coffee, drummed his fingers on the chair arm, removed his glasses, replaced them, jotted notes, then opened his hands. "We have constellated well. We agree that what is missing most is shade. The shade of ancient trees under which Elders gather; the shade cast by older men to nurture younger men; and the transitional shade between darkness and light." He turned to Natalija. "That faint movement of air is always there. Even with facial hair, I can still feel it." He patted both sides of his face. Natalija, smiling, patted her face too.

The Black Magus squinted at the wall clock. "Your writings have been accepted into *The Book of What is Missed*. Now let us look deeper into each."

At 11:01 Jerome and Natalija exited together. Like their previous exit, Jerome wanted to say two things. As before, he led with the one that mattered least. "Have you noticed he rarely uses contractions when he talks?" Natalija half-smiled, her long hair shining in the daylight. He prodded himself to say the second thing.

"So, we 'constellate' well," he said, bracketing constellate in finger quotes. Natalija, cradling her folder, nodded. She looked drained.

"Thank you for your kind words about my poem," she said. "I mean my writing." She lifted and dropped her shoulders and started toward her car. He liked her slender look in worn jeans. But something didn't seem right with her.

"Are you okay?"

"I'm fine," she said over her shoulder. "Thank you for asking."

"Do you have time to stop for coffee? Real coffee?"

Natalija visored her hand across her brow to block sunlight. "Maybe, sometime."

Jerome allowed her to pull out ahead of him. It was just as well she declined his offer. It was likely—from today's writing and her abrupt mood shifts—that she had "issues". He followed her down the drive. She started to turn on to the street then hit the brakes, stopping just before a car sped past. "Easy now," Jerome cautioned. He drummed his fingers on the steering wheel wondering if he should follow to make sure she was okay. Deciding it might be construed as stalking, he pulled onto the street and turned in the opposite direction, toward work.

Chapter 4

The Book of the Sacred

The Drop

Natalija trudged up the stairs and entered her third floor Cleveland Heights apartment. Through an open window rush hour traffic ebbed and flowed between traffic lights on Mayfield Road.

The river of traffic contrasted with the view across the street into a park-like cemetery behind a tall wrought iron fence. When her parents visited, they thought it morbid—having Lakeview cemetery for a neighbor. But this City of the Dead helped calm her, an air of permanent sedation hovering under its luxurious trees. In November, after leaves fell, there was a bonus: the distant blue line of Lake Erie.

She spilled her mail onto her coffee table and noticed an envelope with a handwritten address. Usually anything handwritten came from one of her "ladies" at Heather Hill—a birthday card a week late, or a thank you. Who, she wondered? Mrs. Griffith? Mrs. Mercer? Even though they could hand her the card at work they insisted on mailing, as if to a granddaughter. But the handwriting was too steady for an octogenarian. She opened the envelope and unfolded the lined paper, instantly recognizing the Black Magus' elegant penmanship.

Do not let your hole become too precious!
Fill it as needed
Leaving just enough room
To still reach into
Another world below

Bring back quiet secrets
To the frantic ones above

She walked around the room, circling back to the writing several times to re-read it. She knelt next to the coffee table, clasping her hands under her chin. Another wave of suburban-bound traffic surged below her window. Unlike those commuters, she didn't have a successful job in the city. But none of them ever received mail like this.

Nor did they have her ladies. The women she cared for raved about her. Although appreciated, their sweet chants of praise flowed past her as a pleasant everyday breeze. The real world had taken no notice of her. But someone exceptional had: a well-known published poet. It helped to mitigate the ten-year old catastrophe of dropping out of college.

Refusing to return to Allegheny her sophomore year and being unable to explain why to her parents hadn't seemed like a defeat at the time.

"It will only be for a year. I need to figure some things out." She spent the next several months as a waitress at Ground Round and, on her days off, reading textbooks for the courses she had planned to take that semester as a British Lit. major.

By early February she was missing work days due to a new tiredness which forced her to reduce her waitressing to two nights a week. When her connection to the outside world further shrank to the local library and the uneven bluestone sidewalk between it and her house, her mother intervened.

"Lija, you must go to Vuzenica. I've already discussed it with Aunt Alenka and she is already preparing a room."

She had not been to her mother's hometown in Slovenia since age 10 and always longed to return. But thinking about it now made her even more tired. Why exchange a bedroom here for a bedroom there? But as the date in March approached so did an encouraging notion: she would like it in Slovenia so much that she would stay and find a summer job. And maybe become romantically involved. At her next high school reunion former classmates would remark: "Natty? She's living in Europe."

In late March she arrived in Vuzenica for a six-week visit. What she loved most were Sundays. After mass at St. Nicolas, she, Aunt Alenka and Uncle Oskar joined Cousin Luka's family at a tavern for lunch, and then—after an afternoon hike or card games if it rained—to another tavern for dinner so Aunt Alenka would have a full day's respite from cooking.

But on the last Sunday of her stay in Vuzenica, The Drop occurred.

After Mass, they went to the tavern for lunch. Today was special: "Lija" would be flying back to America in two days. They sat in the garden under a fragrant cherry tree, its blossoms dropping so frequently one landed in her glass of Riesling. Instead of removing it, she took a sip. "It tastes better. I'm serious!" After that, whenever a blossom floated down, every glass lifted to catch it.

Warm sunlight, wine, Luka's dog Ziga sleeping under the table and the beaming affection of her relatives enveloped her. Having achieved, she thought, a perfect moment, something within herself suddenly changed. It started as a sagging of inside weight. Then, internal bindings began snapping, one after the other. She soon lost feeling in her legs. It took several quick glasses of Riesling to suppress rising panic.

After returning to Cleveland it made her nervous to be around other people: they existed in a hyper-reality, faces too bright, voices too loud. Some mornings she never got up, her bedsheets too heavy to push aside.

Trying to understand what had happened, she coined a diagnostic term: *The Drop*. How, on such a beautiful day, blossoms magically falling on their happy party, had she plunged into such a deep abyss? A realization slowly emerged. She had retraced steps to her birth country hoping for something to save her. *The Drop* was the specific moment when she intuitively knew: whatever it was she was searching for did not exist.

Another surge of traffic vibrated against her apartment building and she thought about closing the window. She noticed a pad of paper on a chair, knelt on the floor in front of it and started writing.

And so….
I stopped Entering
Backpedaling instead

She tore out the sheet, balled it and tried to throw it out the open window but it fell short. "Naturally." She turned away. Gazing into the kitchen she noticed her notebook on the table and was reminded she needed to revise her writing for tomorrow's Triangulum meeting. She planned to write the final version with a newly purchased extra fine gel point pen, certain to improve her penmanship. Surely the teacher would notice! "Well, well, missy," she said aloud. "Isn't that interesting." She was looking forward to something in the future. Even if only the next day.

Empty House

Jerome turned into his driveway in Beachwood and pressed the garage door opener. He pulled into the garage, parked, and hit the remote again. The garage door started closing like a heavy curtain on another day's repeat performance. He reflexively went to press the stop engine button but his finger hovered, leaving the car running. The garage door banged shut. Sealed in his garage with the car idling, he looked at the back wall, illuminated by the headlights. *So this would be my last conscious glimpse of life: yard tools.* He shut the car off and quickly pressed the garage door opener. Outdoor light and air filled the garage. His heart pounded. He wondered if he should start parking outside.

His tossed his key fob onto the kitchen counter sending an echo through the nearly empty house. Everyone who knew them thought it odd that Sheri had been the one to move out. But she had never liked the blonde-brick ranch-style home and fled with all of her Herman Miller furniture, leaving only his grandfather's armchair, the object of a pitched battle. Sherri had incessantly argued for its re-upholstering or—even better—disposal. As he walked past the empty chair on his way to collect the mail he patted its high back. "Opa."

He threw the mail on the kitchen counter, instantly recognizing the handwriting on a piece of personal mail. He drummed his fingers on the counter. Why would the Black Magus send him a letter? He could think of only one reason. Despite the other man's ontological bravado, there was something cowardly about him and this is just the way he would terminate someone. Jerome smiled the funny way he did when Sheri told him she wanted a divorce. *I flunked out of a creative writing fellowship where the only other writer is an LPN.* He opened the envelope. Inside were handwritten verses.

Status Quo

Train your eyes
To look for The Opening

It might be a crease of light
Or a black smudge in a brightly-lit office
Sometimes it is in another person's eyes
Or, harder to see
A scratch in their Teflon

When you see it, don't be too tired!
Move closer until you feel its breeze
Like a natural spring bleeding deep water
it comes from a place you cannot see
If unsure, extend your hand
When it disappears, you have found an Opening

Now that you have identified it
Do what you always do:
Note its location and dimensions
So you can circle back
Knowing full well
It will no longer be there

He read it again, re-reading the last stanza a third time. He wasn't sure whether to feel honored or disconcerted. Part of him was pleased the Black Magus had targeted him with special verses. But was it also intended as rapprochement, daring him to *act*? He set the letter down on the granite counter. Noticing breakfast crumbs and a coffee stain, he snatched it back and searched for a cleaner surface.

The Other

From his window chair the Black Magus noted the first red stabs of autumn in maple trees lining the field's wooded fringe to the far left. Years ago he went beyond those trees, descending into a dense ravine. Wanting to re-summon those journeys, he retrieved a favorite scrap from The Reliquary, a green metal strong box used to house his epiphanies: thoughts hastily scrawled onto scraps of paper or index cards. Seeing the lid open one day, Tony had asked:

"Why are you putting your trash in there instead of the waste basket?"

"Its not trash. They are glowing embers from my unconscious."

The box also included several keepsakes his sister Rachel had not taken—his father's Silver Star earned at the Battle of the Bulge, one of his mother's rosaries, and a few photographs. On top of the box Tony facetiously taped an index card labelled "My Reliquary". The Black Magus liked the sacramental analogy and kept it, marking out "My" and substituting "The".

He reached in and withdrew a scrap of paper. It had been handled so often it drooped across is fingers.

From the field edge above, sunlight
angles between darkened tree trunks
Out of breath, I reach for a slanting beam
And pull myself up to the brightening rim
Hand over hand

On that particular day he had crossed the field and ventured into the steep ravine with a collapsible chair and thermos of cold gin. Halfway down the wooded slope he found a level spot and, scuffing up earth smells, pressed the chair legs into deep loam. At the bottom of the ravine a silver ribbon of water slipped over green rocks; he liked that it was analogous to the gin slipping icily down his gullet. Draining the thermos, inertness rose from his legs and, reaching his head, merged him with the forest's dappled light.

Was it enough to camouflage him for the encounter he had come for? Masking consciousness, could he lure An Other into the open? Would it be a fox? A rare bird? Maybe even a bobcat.

But the woods were deathly silent. So still he could feel its slow-motion suction: the dragging under of surface matter into the devouring anaerobic machine below the matted leaves. Soon he felt tiny pricks on his sockless ankles but, upon inspection, detected nothing. The prickling continued and finally he knew: his camouflage was so effective the forest floor was mistaking him for something dead. With piranha-like precision it was gnawing his bare ankles.

He recapped the thermos, re-slung the chair, and faced back up the steep slope.

Recalling the episode engendered mixed feelings. He had failed to lure An Other. But redemption occurred on the climb out: a rope of light angling down through the trees. Pulling himself out of the ravine into the sunlit field was a small rebirthing. To this day he was certain he had held a sunbeam in his hands, fingers gripping a silken cord sheathed in golden light.

When he first told Tony about it, he already knew his friend's response:

"Hallucinogen Persisting Perception Disorder. You dropped enough window pane back-in-the day to kill a blue whale."

Sipping coffee and savoring the morning light through his back window, he laid the scrap of paper aside. Suddenly, he set down his coffee as if too hot and slapped his face. "Idiot! You completely missed it!"

He had waited in the ravine for An Other to appear. But he thought It would be warm-blooded—a fox, a bobcat; something sexy in the "rare-sighting" category. But he had been sitting above it the whole time: the microbial swarm quivering beneath the forest floor. Equating it with mosquitos, he had fled.

He stared out the window across the field toward the trees which marked the ravine's edge. "Is it too late to go back?" Even if able to descend the ravine, would there be a sunbeam powerful enough to winch his aging hulk back up? Or would he remain trapped below the brightening rim, to die from exposure. To finally merge with The Other.

Second Meeting of the Tenth Triangulum

Jerome paused at the end of the driveway. It was 9:59am and he could see Natalija's parked Corolla. Aware of his aloofness during the two prior sessions, today he felt vulnerable.

At the end of last week's session the Black Magus asked them to bring writings for *The Book of the Sacred.* Jerome asked for clarity: "Sacred in a religious sense? Or secular?"

"What is sacred to you?" the Black Magus had replied. "Or what is sacred to us? Is there even such a thing anymore?"

It didn't help that Natalija rejoiced at the topic. "Oh, good! I have something in mind." Throughout his adult life Jerome knew he had sidestepped the sacred as a concept. The closest he had come to experiencing it was when, as a law student, he worked a summer at Jones Day. On his first day he encountered Werner, the imposing, silver-haired senior partner, in the men's room. He was so flummoxed by the other man's unsmiling omnipotence that he stood at the adjacent urinal unable to initiate small talk, or urine.

Entering the Black Magus' front room he expected to find Natalija vanquished from failed chit chat. Instead she and their host energetically conversed about cats. The instant Jerome sat, the Black Magus stopped talking and donned his reading glasses. To mask his uneasiness, Jerome launched a diversionary attack. "How did you become the Black Magus?"

Natalija's head went up. The large man squinted sharply. "Why do *you* think I am called that?"

"Before I met you....I thought maybe you were black."

"I thought that too," Natalija added.

"Do you still think that?"

Jerome realized he had to tread carefully. "You do bear a resemblance to Wolf Man Jack." He turned to Natalija. "Have you ever seen the 1960s movie American Graffiti?" She shook her head. He looked at the Black Magus' swarthy arms which he judged lighter than Wolfman Jack's. "People can have....percentages."

The Black Magus removed his glasses and rubbed his eyes. "In the 1980s I wrote my only novel. An editor at Holt, after apologizing for rejecting it, wrote that one of the characters, The Black Magus, said extraordinary things." He paused. "It was the only compliment my stillborn novel ever received."

"Do you still have the manuscript?" Natalija asked.

"I burned it." The Black Magus smiled. "Except for one character."

He replaced his glasses and gazed at the open folder in his lap. "Today, we bring writings to the *Book of The Sacred.* The sacred is something I still struggle to define." He distributed his handwritten sheets. "What I bring."

Locked In

We know we are getting closer to the sacred
When we want to start crawling

It is why old people tilt lower
Bent devotionally towards death

And why at Canterbury
Centuries of pilgrim's bony knees

Carved a depression up marble stairs
vectoring
For the Martyr's bones

If someone had yelled "fire"
They could not have run

In pre-dawn darkness
A man prostrates himself in front of an Apple store
Trembling
For the Next Coming

When the doors open
He starts crawling

If someone yells fire
He cannot run

Natalija rocked excitedly. "I also allude to a cathedral."

The Black Magus arched his brows as if a little girl had run up to him with something in her hand. "Show us what you bring." Natalija handed out copies of her writing.

The Beam

Have you sensed The Beam?

It comes down at a slant
as if through a high Cathedral window
Light so pure
It is almost blue

If close enough
it might graze your shoulder
making you mutter:
What just touched me?

Tracking like a stage light
it knows where you are going.
When you veer right
it is already turning
But if you are too full
how can it enter?

Stop veering
Stand still
Hold out your hand
for a bird to alight

Jerome was the first to weigh in. "Its spooky. But in a good way. An ethereal way."

The Black Magus massaged his jaw. "Why a beam of light from above? It is so metaphysically trite."

Natalija's face fell. Jerome's lawyerly instincts kicked in. He addressed the Black Magus. "I think you're making too much of the beam itself. It effectively sets us up for the last two lines, 'Hold out your hand, For a bird to alight'. What's most important is pausing to receive."

"But why a bird?" The Black Magus asked.

"A symbol of the spirit."

The Black Magus grimaced. "A cliché of the spirit. Why does *The Other* have to be furry or feathery? A bob-cat or a bird? Why not an enzyme?"

Jerome re-read Natalija's writing. "Where does she reference a Bob-cat? And did you say enzyme?"

The Black Magus extended a conciliatory hand toward Natalija. "What you brought is very good. I projected a personal setback into it. I once overrated a sunbeam and now it is a thorn."

Natalija leaned forward over her crossed legs. "Would it help to talk about it?"

The Black Magus gazed between them. "It doesn't have to come from above. If you feel a tickle on your bare ankles, it has alighted."

Jerome twisted his mouth, wanting to challenge the Black Magus' obtuseness. Instead, he nervously scanned his own writing for An Other. The Black Magus prodded him. "What do you bring to *The Book of the Sacred*?"

"Good question."

"Shush," the Black Magus cautioned. Jerome reluctantly distributed his writing to their waiting hands.

First Lemonade

My womb-memory is not as powerful
as for some

the addicts
who once they taste a way
to recall original wholeness
destroy themselves to feel it
again and again

Sometimes it can be safely glimpsed
Many say this happens during lovemaking
But the best moment is
immediately <u>after,</u> when

all doors and windows, having blown open
allow in sunlight and warm breezes

When vivid enough, our eyes moisten

bodies quivering
for that first lemonade

Jerome gripped the back of his neck. The last line still bothered him. Lemonade seemed like a stock image from a Norman Rockwell painting.

Natalija moved a finger across each line. "I think Jerome says it best. All doors and windows must be blown open. Only then can *it* enter. Or alight. Or tickle. Or make us want to crawl." She leaned sideways toward Jerome and, making a clicking sound inside her cheek, gave him a thumbs-up.

The Black Magus closed his eyes. "Change 'first lemonade' to upper case," he said. "It is that important." He bounced his fingertips together. "I *see* things. I am not as good at tasting, hearing, or touching." He opened his eyes and turned to Jerome. "Thank you,"

"For what?" Jerome said, half-opening his hands. The sacred was his weakest subject. Yet he was being thanked for what he had written.

"You helped me identify what I quiver for when I gaze into the deep pond."

Natalija scrunched forward. "The Deep Translucent Pond?"

The Black Magus' flinched. "It's strange to hear someone else say that."

Natalija turned to Jerome. "He's an artist too. There's a drawing in his bathroom. You should go look."

Jerome nodded but wasn't sure where this was heading.

Natalija, hands clasped on her lap, coyly leaned toward the Black Magus. "What is the Deep Translucent Pond? Can you tell us?"

The Black Magus stared at the floor. After several nostril contractions and expansions he muttered: "A great mystery. No. A great thirst." His right hand, lifting from the chair arm, began to rhythmically open and close as if trying to grip something.

"Your hand is doing something," Jerome observed.

The Black Magus pointed at the floor. "There, at the bottom! Don't you see?" Jerome and Natalija looked down and, seeing only worn green carpet, lifted their eyes in concern. The Black Magus' eyes fluttered and he looked back and forth between his two students. "Perhaps the three of us together will have a reach long enough!"

Natalija tilted her head quizzically, then turned to Jerome. "I think it would help if we were all familiar with the drawing. Go look. In the bathroom. It's very good."

Jerome smiled. "I'm sure I'll make it in there." A few minutes ago the teacher had complimented his writing and he was inclined to let him off Natalija's hook. Besides, there was no precedent in his life for what she was asking him to do. He had never visited someone's bathroom to view original artwork and saw no reason to start now.

Chapter 5

The Book of Slow Leaks

Hyper-Space

Jerome met Phil Lundy for coffee at Lakeland Community College where, as professor emeritus in Humanities, he still taught one class. He led Jerome up a spiral staircase to the cafeteria's mezzanine level. His long wavy white hair and thick black-framed eyeglasses seemed to blend his dual identities as academic and poet. They sat at a table near a wall of windows, the outside light suffusing green through a thick lens of tree canopies.

Jerome lifted his coffee toward the window. "Very scenic." At that moment a young woman in tight pants brushed past their table. "The outside view, I meant."

Phil, occupied with prying the lid from his coffee, winced from the steam. "How are things going?"

"He *is* an acquired taste."

"His brilliance is only exceeded by his eccentricities."

"He never refers to his past fame."

Phil blew on his coffee. "I think he's bored with the ego. Not just his own, but the mere concept of it."

"So you two have been friends since high school? What was he like?"

"When we were seniors, my dad brought back a pack of Gauloises cigarettes from France. When he finished the pack, I retrieved it from a waste basket, filled it with Winstons, and my senior year persona was set. But compared to Bear I was playacting. While I thought I was pretty superior reading *Zen and the Art of Motorcycle Maintenance,* Bear was devouring Nietzsche. He was way ahead of us all. I mean, prodigy. An unlikely cross between Jim Morrison and Jean Paul Sartre. The summer after we graduated I came across him one night at the Euclid Tavern. He was catatonically stoned; didn't even recognize me. The next day he was sitting cross-legged in Cain Park leading a circle discussion on Kierkegaard".

Jerome sipped coffee. *Bear.* Though only a high school nickname, he felt he had unearthed an interesting artifact relating to the Black Magus' early life. "What about d. a. levy? What was it like between them?"

"They didn't know each other half as well as local literary lore would have it. Bear was younger and a late arrival to the 60s scene. d.a. was a kind of John-the-Baptist action figure paving the way, the Poet-Provocateur par excellence. Bear succeeded him as the Poet-Philosopher. He never served a day in jail for obscene literature, like d.a. Was never really into the so-called 'mimeograph revolution' that galvanized the local scene. He was always about permanence, the eternal. But as the two most famous Cleveland poets of a generation their names are forever linked. Though d.a. still gets more attention."

"I would think committing suicide at age 26 helps with that."

"When d.a. killed himself in '68," —Phil pointed to a spot between his eyes—' a bullet to third eye in the lotus position'—it cratered Cleveland's arts community. Bear helped fill the void when—a the year later, still at Kent State—his first book of poems was published.

"Lemming Song?

"In 1970 he churned out his second book, *The Distant Sound of Heaven*. That one got national attention. When Allen Ginsburg came to Cleveland in '71 they did a reading together at The Gate Coffeehouse. The line was out the door."

"What led to his….." Jerome slowly twirled a hand.

"Breakdown?" Phil massaged his jaw. "He held steady until '74, published two more volumes, then called me one day to announce he was hitch-hiking to California. He said he didn't want to end up like d.a.. I figured he meant dead before age 30. The cool destination was still San Francisco, so of course he went to LA. He shacked up with a black woman 15 years older, did a fair amount of LSD and Mescaline, and didn't write a damn thing. After gestating for nine months and no rebirth to show for it—his words, from a poem—he fled back to Cleveland. By Greyhound. Somewhere in Iowa he hit the hyper-space button. He became convinced the other riders were plotting to kill him, so he started to threaten them. The Sioux City police took him off the bus in handcuffs."

"Hyper-space button?"

"Its from a 1970s video game. Asteroids? Maybe it's still around. You're about to collide with something that's going to obliterate you so, as a last resort, you hit the hyperspace button and randomly land somewhere else. It could be a better spot. Or worse."

"Which was it for him?"

Phil Lundy shrugged. "It kept him above ground. Albeit with severe limitations."

"I only remember hearing about him as a recluse."

"After Iowa he was diagnosed as a paranoid schizophrenic. Except for occasional stints in a psyche hospital, he barely left his house. After his mother died it was just him and his dad, a gregarious alcoholic. I persuaded him to come to a 20 year anniversary reading of *Lemming Song* in '89. It was standing room only. Myself and a few other old hippies performed the readings. Following that event, he started attending the League's monthly workshops. I'd pick him up and another high school chum, Tony, took him home. At one workshop someone criticized his new stuff as too didactic, so he stopped coming."

"Was it didactic?"

"I call it his 'Thus Spake Zarathustra phase'. Penetrating stuff but spewed with a flame thrower. He argued that flame throwers had a place in poetry. That's when he started signing everything 'The Black Magus'."

"The Triangulum—I mean the Fellowship Project—how did that come about?"

"In the 90s he volunteered to lead a creative writing workshop at Hill House, a program for mentally ill adults trying to re-enter the flow. His goal was to help them, quote, "repair their damaged psyches through writing". I sat in on a workshop. Despite his brusqueness, they loved him."

Jerome stared at sugar granules on the table. Did the Black Magus take him on as a pupil because he perceived a "damaged psyche"?

Phil resumed. "Hill House re-ignited skills from the Cain Park days. He remembered he could teach. Facilitate. When Hill House shut down, he slipped back under his rock. I stopped by one day and told him he was a still a damn good poet but also a damn good teacher and needed to keep sharing both gifts. It took some doing, but I was able to finagle an honorarium from the Literary League for the fellowship project."

"Ten years is an amazing run. The eighteen poetry fellows who preceded us must be bugging the hell out of you, wanting to know if this thing will ever get published."

Phil arched a grey brow above his black glass frames. "Strangely, no. Nobody's ever pestered me. If the subject comes up—and usually I'm the one broaching it—I brace for flak but they all just kind of do this....little smile." Phil paused to sip coffee. "So, you and Natalija are the final two. How's she doing?"

"Seems to be into it," Jerome replied.

"She's got immense upside potential. I'd like her to apply to CSU's creative writing program."

Jerome wondered if Phil felt similarly about his abilities. He had planned to ask him about graduate programs in creative writing but changed his mind. "After the project ends, what do you think he'll do?"

"He'll only surrender the fellowship manuscripts if I back down his driveway in a Brink's truck. They will get modestly published in a chapbook series and The Literary League will have a special unveiling with wine and cheese which he may or may not attend. After that....." He looked at Jerome, his grey eyes uncertain. A student with a greasy wedge of pizza sat down at an adjacent table. Phil grimaced. "Tomato sauce doesn't complement my morning coffee". He pushed his chair back to get up. "When's your next session?"

"Tomorrow. The Book of Slow Leaks."

Quiet Secrets

When Natalija arrived at work, she was happy to see that her favorite tree, an ancient Sugar Maple, was fringing red. It was always the first tree to change. Gazing at its scarlet leaf tips, she recited lines from the writing the Black Magus had mailed her several weeks ago, now her morning mantra:

Bring back quiet secrets
to the frantic ones above

She smiled at the tree. "You're one of my quiet secrets. But how do I bring you back?"

It concerned her, sometimes, that she had worked at the assisted care facility long enough to have a favorite tree. Although Heather Hill had not cured her depression, it had given her a reason to push her bedsheets aside each morning. She had, in fact, hardly missed a day since completing her LPN four years ago.

It had been her mother's idea—shocked by her daughter's deepening depression after returning from Slovenia—for her to accompany a parish outreach group to Heather Hill. It was there she discovered something about herself: she could make old people smile. Like the old books she lovingly borrowed from the library, the old people collected dust in a repository. Weekly volunteer visits to the facility led her to a new, menial purpose: brushing dust from slumping shoulders.

She completed the nursing assistant program in 16 weeks and was immediately hired. Two years later she became an LPN. Every charge nurse she worked with encouraged her to enter an RN program, but she drew a line. "If I move up, I won't get to spend as much time with my ladies."

Today there was one lady she especially wanted to see. After report, she entered Room 8. "Do you have any quiet secrets, Dorothy?" she asked, opening the blinds. She went over to the frail, snowy-haired woman in the bed. Mrs. Huffnagel tried to smile through a pained look. "What's wrong, my love?" Natalija asked, stroking the old woman's white hair.

"I was so worried about you," Mrs. Huffnagel whispered.

"Why were you worried?"

Mrs. Huffnagel smiled, seeming to forget why she was worried. "You're so beautiful."

Natalija leaned over and kissed her forehead. "Every morning you make my day." She squeezed Mrs. Huffnagel's soft hand then elevated the upper part of the bed to bend her upright. "Time for breakfast. Promise me you'll eat everything?"

Mrs. Huffnagel's eyes fluttered ambiguously.

As Natalija left the room she felt a dark unease. Mrs. Huffnagel had barely eaten anything, solid or soft, for a week. But the look in her eyes, which she had seen in other ladies no longer here, disturbed her most: Mrs. Huffnagel had decided it was time to go. She paused at the door and bit her lip. She would personally bring Mrs. Huffnagel's tray and feed her herself.

Ten minutes later Natalija returned with breakfast. "Oatmeal, with brown sugar! Your favorite, Dorothy!" She placed the tray on the table and, about to swivel it over, noticed Mrs. Huffnagel had closed her eyes. "Dorothy, you promised." Mrs. Huffnagel didn't respond. Her complexion had changed. Natalija gently shook her. "Dorothy!" Natalija reflexively pressed two fingers above the woman's wrist. Still warm. But no pulse. She pressed an ear against her chest. Silence. She felt no breath against her upturned ear.

Natalija half-sat on the edge of the bed and clamped her hands to her cheeks. Like the maple tree, Mrs. Huffnagel had been in the same place every morning when she arrived. The old tree greeted her with its seasonal changes. The old woman with a smile. Natalija closed her eyes, squeezing out tears. Mrs. Huffnagel was gone. And all her quiet secrets with her.

Visitation

Never before had the Night Daemon attempted to communicate with him. About to swat the pesky intruder off his chest, something stopped the Black Magus—the rubbery smell of Ked's high top sneakers.

He knew the smell from childhood. But why was he smelling it now? As his eyes got used to the dark he could make out a shadowy figure sitting cross-legged on his chest, the figure's crossed ankles thrust slightly forward so that the tips of his shoes—high top sneakers—grazed either side of the Black Magus' chin. He couldn't recall the daemon ever wearing anything; only its weight. Now it seemed to be wearing something all the same color, like a jumpsuit.

The daemon bent over and softly lisped in his ear: "Something is building." Wispy beard hairs tickled his cheek.

The Black Magus lunged for the bedside lamp, almost knocking it over. After propping himself he waited for his frantic breathing to subside. It was the first time the Daemon had spoken to him. The voice, the sneakers, even the thin beard, were new, though somehow familiar. He grabbed his yellow pad and started writing.

Something is building!
Green lawns hot as asphalt
From something stabbing upward

What will it be like
When the surface finally breaks?
Will it be fun to watch,
Or will it destroy the land?

A dragon in the sky
Can be seen and shot at

For the dragon breathing beneath us
It makes no sense
To shoot at the ground

He re-read it, surprised it had gushed into readable verse. Could the Daemon—or whoever it was—have guided his hand? Knowing the trickster could steal it back, he slipped the pad under his pillow. The next morning it was still there.

Later that day, while Tony helped him put away groceries, the Black Magus abruptly turned to his friend. "Did you ever hear d.a. levy talk?"

Tony, his long grey locks in a pony tail, lifted his brow. "Couple of times. At that bookstore where they did the readings. Asphoedel?"

"What do you remember about his voice?"

Tony, stacking Campbell soup cans, reflected. "It wasn't what you'd expect from his bad boy reputation. Thin, soft. Kinda lispy."

"Yes, I remember that," the Black Magus replied, comparing it to the voice that spoke to him during the night.

"I remember," Tony continued, "goin' to one of his readings right after he got outta jail. When he walked in he got a standing ovation. He was wearin' a jumpsuit, like in jail, and black hightop sneakers. He had that beatnik beard—a bit on the wimpy side I always thought."

The box of Bisquick the Black Magus was putting away slipped from his hand, tumbling into the sink, taking a jar of Sanka with it. The Black Magus flattened his hands on the counter and stared straight down.

"You okay?" Tony asked, striding over to retrieve the tumbled groceries.

"I had a disturbing night."

"You mean a normal night."

After Tony left, he re-read the cryptic jotting from the previous night. *Yes, I can see d.a.'s hand in this. But why? I already have a daemon I'm accustomed to.* He handwrote "daemon" then underlined the first two letters, a "d" and an "a". A coincidence?

Re-examining the jotting he found its message depressing. Either his paranoid delusions were returning, or some kind of world collapse was approaching. Or both.

To calm himself he went to the back room, sat in the window chair and retrieved a writing from The Reliquary. Weakened from over-handling, the paper draped over his hand.

Re-Enchantment

Infuse me
Fill me with your ancient breath
Bleed the spent black fluid
hot from my ears
Let it run thick and rancid
Collapsing my starched white collar

Jab me with your wand
Strike open my eyes
Make me see:
The aura around every living thing
The energy pulsing between stars
The gods racing along a burning cloud edge
Your slender, gentle, motioning arm

Finally, at twilight, beneath old trees:
The Deep Translucent Pond
From the bottom, old swords glimmer
Relics
of an earlier light

The last stanza remained an enigma. When the pond first appeared in a dream he equated its steep sides with the quarry.

He had thought it an unconscious attempt to work through his cowardice in not letting go of the rope. But in subsequent dreams, or sometimes through actively imagining himself there, the pond transformed.

The breakthrough dream occurred sixteen years ago.

Stars ornamented the tree canopies above, enough to guide him between ancient tree trunks. Entering the clearing, he expected to encounter the steep sided quarry. But this time the water was flush with the ground, a floating circular pond radiating submerged light. At its grassy edge he gazed into water clear and still. It seemed miles deep, the bottom glittering as if from a million goldfish scales. He marveled that light could come from such a deep place.

But its translucence was a changeable lens. Staring at the deep glitter, the bottom lifted towards him, the tiny scintilla magnifying into a shimmering carpet of medieval broadswords. All the blades were broken, dismembered from their hilts, many into smaller pieces. Except for one which lay casually atop the broken ones. Spotting it, his right twitched to grip it, opening and closing. He felt a painful thirst, his tongue a dry rag, making him want to drop onto his stomach and, lapping like a dog, drink the entire pond. But something about the water frightened him. It was almost too placid. Like the cooling pool of a reactor.

The morning after the dream he woke up and wrote *Re-enchantment*. It had taken years for the imaginal pond to fill, for the water to clear. Surely the dream and resulting poem represented a psychic mending within himself.

On that day he felt an energy toward the world he hadn't known since before his breakdown. When Tony called to ask if he wanted anything from the grocery store he asked to come along. Later he dug up the phone number for the director of the Creative Writing Program at Cleveland State and left her a voicemail, asking if the writer-in-residence fellowship she offered him four years ago was still available. He even picked up fallen branches from his front yard and waved at one of his new neighbors.

But as the week progressed his re-unified Self atrophied. When Tony asked if he wanted to go to the library he said no. A dog barking across the field made him kick a door and scrounge for ear plugs. He never heard back from Cleveland State. By Friday he wouldn't get out of bed, and he knew why. He had stumbled upon a hideout of the fugitive gods. *BUT NOT YET THEM*!

Since then, the pond was frustratingly inscrutable. *If the pond is so deep, why can I sometimes see the bottom? Why are the swords broken, except for one? Am I right to call it ancient light?* For the past year he had given up re-visiting the pond at all. But because of something one of his pupil's brought to last week's Triangulum meeting, he decided it was time to re-enter the image. He pulled down the window shade and closed his eyes.

Emerging from the woods into the pond's deep glow he felt the same quivering thirst as before. This time he knew why. "That First Lemonade", he croaked, recalling Jerome's words. He entered the light and gazed into the pond. Rather than allow himself to be mesmerized, he looked away. He had never paid attention to the area surrounding the pond and this time he would. His face cooled as if turned from a campfire.

The pond's grassy perimeter was starkly vacant. It had always seemed normal that he was the only one there. But now his aloneness struck him. *Where are the others to bask in this deep light?* His right hand started to twitch, gripping and re-gripping air. Could a hand have its own ancient memories? What was it trying to say? He turned back to the pond and extended his twitching right hand. The water cleared and the swords appeared.

But I cannot reach that deep! He lifted his gaze and surveyed the desolate grassy perimeter. A voice sounded in his head. "Bring others to this edge. Together you will have an arm long enough."

The Black Magus opened his eyes. "Yes, yes. The way is clearer." He even knew who the others would be. The Tenth Triangulum might be the last; but it was fated for something higher.

Feeling he had achieved another breakthrough, he celebrated with his daily cigarette. Exhaling a plume, he closed his eyes. "Pray that I am not too late, mother. Or too old." His face tightened then slowly relaxed. He resolutely lifted his chin. "Something is building. New warriors must be trained."

Third Meeting of the Tenth Triangulum

As Natalija turned onto the worn gravel drive, she felt the usual mix of excitement and dread.

The Black Magus sometimes reminded her of Ms. Bell, her sixth grade teacher. Unsmiling, no-nonsense Ms. Bell was capable of astonishing moments of empathy. Especially on those dreaded days when students had to give reports in front of the class.

Quaking at her desk, awaiting her turn, she remembered how Ms. Bell would come alongside, lean over and whisper: "When you're up there, just look at me." As she trembled in front of her classmates unable to speak, she would look at Ms. Bell, beaming and nodding from her desk in the corner. The words would come. She sometimes wondered if she was the only one who ever saw Ms. Bell smile.

She wasn't nervous to speak now. But bringing a piece of her soul to be critiqued each week was hard. The Black Magus seemed to intuit when she was on the brink. "*You see that door? It will never close on your fingers*." And it hadn't. He didn't have Ms. Bell's secret smile. But like her, he knew.

As she pulled up, Jerome, wearing a blue blazer over a pale yellow dress shirt, emerged from his Audi, his dark hair bending in the breeze. "A handsome lawyer is waiting for you," she said aloud, testing the words' effect. Glancing in the rearview mirror she saw she was blushing.

After parking, she got out and came alongside Jerome. A breeze ruffled the omnipresent driveway puddles. Jerome smiled. "Did you bring your slow leaks?"

"Well.....I brought me." Jerome reached out intending to pat her on the shoulder, then retracted his arm. At that moment his cell phone rang. "I better get this."

Natalija proceeded to the house where she knocked, then entered. The Black Magus' was nowhere to be seen. "Hello", she called out. The room seemed brighter. A door, usually closed, opened to an adjacent back room just before the hallway. She maneuvered for a better look, noticing a wooden chair facing out an unadorned window. Curious, she started to cut through the triangle defined by the chairs, stopped halfway, backpedaled, and instead circumnavigated the triangle to get to the back room. When she was almost to the doorway, the Black Magus emerged from the hallway to the right. He ambled in front of her and shut the door, extinguishing her view into the room.

"There was such a pleasant light coming from in there," Natalija said.

The Black Magus, smelling of minty toothpaste, scrutinized her peripherally. "What kind of light?" He reached for the doorknob, froze, then glanced at the wall clock. "It is 9:59." He pointed his cane toward the chairs.

Jerome arrived a minute later and took his assigned seat. "Present," he said, half-raising a hand.

The Black Magus brought his fingertips together. "I was unusually vague about this week's topic, but—as you know by now—I don't wish to constrict." He turned to Jerome. "The last shall be first. What do you bring to *The Book of Slow Leaks?"*

Jerome wished he hadn't taken the call from the office. Though it had been unimportant, he felt tainted and needed more time to transition. "In preparing for this, it occurred to me that a slow leak can't be an object because an object is lost instantly. Or..."

The Black Magus held up a hand to pause him. "What do you bring?"

Jerome obediently handed out his handwritten copies.

The Great Dissolving

Each day losing more to the solvent of time
Not a washing away,
but a fine mist rivuletting into vital substance
carrying away parts of me too
small to measure.
Each month, each year
new sediment layers form
core samples of my life
the earliest thick and petrified
later ones still cooling
no longer molten
no longer flowing
Deadening into cold strata

The Black Magus contemplated the ceiling. "My first thought is always a birth-edge response." He interlocked his fingers, jutting an index finger at Jerome. "You like to think there are neat horizontal divisions measuring your life. You are probably fascinated by cross-sections of trees that have been cut down. You like counting the growth rings."

Jerome's eyes enlarged. On his patio was a thirty-inch slice of tree trunk which had been re-purposed into a three-legged table. He had applied the high-gloss polyurethane to its surface himself.

The Black Magus continued. "I am concerned about certain words". He read from his pad: "....cooling, no longer flowing, deadening, cold, sediment...."

"What is your concern?" Jerome interrupted.

The Black Magus turned to Natalija. "Your thoughts?"

Natalija silently re-read it, moving her finger line by line. "There is a slowing. A hardening."

"A petrifaction," the Black Magus added.

"Sounds like criticism," Jerome snapped, "of a personal nature."

The Black Magus opened his hands. "If you are going to think of your life in geologic terms, then include an active volcano. Go to the crater's edge and look in. Stand there until the soles of your shoes melt. Stop being mesmerized by watching your life congeal and harden."

Jerome stiffened. "So I should accept your acidic remarks as a teaching moment?"

The Black Magus' frowned. "Open your hands!" Jerome hesitated, then complied. The Black Magus shifted forward to examine them. "I want to see calluses. From rowing. At the end of this Triangulum, I want to exam your hands again." He turned to the side table and jotted on his yellow pad.

Jerome, still holding out his hands, appealed to Natalija for interpretation.

"It's good, what you wrote," she said.

"For a geologist," he mouthed. Natalija placed her hands on her hips, elbows out, mimicking a scolding mother. The Black Magus turned to her.

"What is it you bring to *The Book of Slow Leaks*?"

Natalija handed out her sheet.

Trickling Out

No more classes or books
on how to mindfully pause.
What interests me is being able to say:
"I am full!"

Not an after-dinner paralytic full
But a percolating over-ripeness
pushing to spill over

No, not in a sap-flowing goatish way!
But a slow filling, upward seeping
Which, when the basin fills
trickles free
to join other streams

The Black Magus swept his arms upward, pantomiming an updraft. "There is a bringing up, a filling, and then a branching. The three essential actions of being. The last cannot happen without the first two."

"Oh," Natalija said, startled. "Thank you. But isn't Jerome saying the same thing in the first part of his writing?" She lifted his writing and read aloud.

"Not a washing away
but a fine mist rivuletting
into vital substance
carrying away parts of me
too small to measure"

Natalija extended her arm and unfurled her slender fingers. "It was easier to focus on the second part of his writing—the calcifying part, or whatever you called it. But in the first part something is flowing. From *Him*."

The Black Magus spread his fingers braille-like over Jerome's writing. "He does speak to the paradox of moisture—life-giving vs. destroying." He held out his right hand toward Jerome and, palm facing down, pantomimed a patting motion. "Stone is porous. Pat your hand against one in the morning and you can feel it drinking the morning dew. Anything that holds moisture can replenish." He opened his arms to both students. "What matters is outward flow. Spreading your rich alluvial selves across the land."

Jerome blinked at the reversal. He turned to Natalija and their eyes met. She tilted her head, green eyes smiling. Jerome looked down and shook his head, pantomiming remorse for his earlier touchiness.

The Black Magus passed out his sheet. "What I bring."

Winter Draw

Low sun through frozen trees
With each barefoot step across the snowy field
The quiet cold
Draws blackness from my bones

Is it considerate to leave such a sooty trail
Absorbed into cotton purity?

Keep going:
Toxins distilled this way
Will settle during the next thaw
And then
        the rains

For some reason Jerome was reminded of a winter afternoon in Helja, running from a sauna with other men, naked bodies expelling steamy plumes against a huge orange sun. Resting the writing on his crossed right leg, he waggled his pen. "Your leaking is more of a purge."

"As opposed to alluvial," Natalija added.

The Black Magus removed his glasses and rubbed his eyes. "I am presuming the earth can absorb my toxins. There are days when I could poison the whole planet." He breathed heavily through his nose, building toward a pronouncement. "As a society we connote leaks as negative. But it is clear from today's writings that a slow leak can be beneficial: an outward rivuletting of self, or....a purging of something black." The Black Magus took off his glasses, tilted his head back and gazed at the ceiling. "Natalija brought to light an undervalued word: alluvial."

"No, *you* said alluvial," Natalija corrected. She read from her notes. "'Rich alluvial selves'".

"Whomever," the Black Magus said. "Let us discuss alluvial. Not as a word, but as a vital component of being."

Chapter 6

The Book of Lightness

Waking Before Birth

Natalija knew the time without looking: 3am.

Almost every night it was the same: fully awake at 3am, fiery fragments from the previous day bombarding her skull. If, by 4:30, she failed to find sleep again, she would drag herself into the kitchen, sit back from the glare of the street light and await morning. The worst moment actually came when dawn light strengthened through the window and she knew she would miss out on waking up.

An unsettling thought emerged: was her 3am insomnia a nightly re-enactment of her birth? Instead of awakening in a birthing room 30 years ago, maybe she had already been awake in her mother's womb, awaiting her first tunneled glimpse of light. How much better it would have been to awaken outside the womb. Like everyone else.

"That's it," she said aloud. "I lack a sense of having been born."

She thought of the day ahead. At 10am she would sit in one of three chairs in a famous poet's living room. She was one complete side of an isosceles triangle. Whether she regained sleep or not, in several hours she would become an integral part of the most stable shape.

She rolled on her side, closed her eyes, and imagined lying inside a one-person pyramid with thick plexi-glass sides. To test its strength she imagined sledge hammers glancing noiselessly off the slanted sides. Intrigued, she transported her portable pyramid to a pebbly ocean shore. Curled inside, she watching at eye level as violent waves slammed into the slanted wall inches from her face. When her pyramidal beach hut started to shake, she spoke the words Sister Ann Marie suggested during the first months of The Drop: *Hold me, Jesus.... Calm me, Jesus....Love me, Jesus.*

Weaving the words into a relaxing cadence, the waves began to slacken. The last thing she remembered before falling back to sleep were defeated wisps of foam.

Validation

Jerome liked to read in bed before turning off the light, a habit Sheri never liked. "My father used to read in bed. I don't like that you remind me of my father."

He remembered being concerned in their courting days that she didn't read books, only legal briefs. Later he identified it as one of the early signs of a fungus: one of the innate differences that had, during their five years together, spread undetected. His marriage ended not because of a fracture, but because of dry rot.

His head propped against the headboard by pillows, he felt himself getting sleepy and set down the book on World War II he was reading. Too tired to reach for the light, an image of Sheri suddenly intruded. He threw off the covers, whirled his legs over the edge of the bed and opened the small drawer on the bedside table. Empty orange prescription bottles with the name Sheri

Griesmer on the label tumbled forward. He had never thought to throw out the bottles thinking she had kept them for some reason and might ask for them—one never knew with her. Now, over a year later, they survived as rare artifacts of the person who had once slept on that side of the bed.

His first image of her eight years ago flashed: a self-possessed, attractive brunette peering over neon blue eyeglass frames as she presented an impeccable PowerPoint at a legal seminar. How had an average-looking guy like him ever scored that? She had been impressed with his Ivy League credentials, his apparent upward trajectory in a prestigious firm, and—he had good reason to believe—his intelligence. What changed during marriage? His undergraduate and law degrees hadn't changed nor, he hoped, his intelligence. But in the firm's increasing use of metrics to rate individual performance, his upward trajectory had not fared as well. *What the hell—I was still a Partner. Still am.*

From the back of the tiny drawer he pulled three more artifacts, ones *he* had put there: valentine's cards she had given him their first three years of marriage. All three had fuzzy textured red hearts like the best ones from childhood, the handwriting on each card saying the same thing: "Love You, – Sherri." Pain slanted across his chest and stomach. *How could this be? How could someone who no longer wants to know me have written this?*

He yanked out the drawer, got up, and strode from the room. It was best to dispose of the drawer's contents in the greasy kitchen trash from which he would be less tempted to retrieve them. He pushed the foot pedal of the trash bin and turned the drawer upside down. As the pill bottles tumbled into the trash, at the last second he reached in to the upturned drawer to secure the valentines. He returned to his bedroom, sat on the edge of the bed and slid the drawer back into the bedside table. It made him feel weak, that he couldn't part with the cards. And, like so many times before, he knew why. If he were to die in this house alone, then whoever sorted his things would come across documentation that he had once been loved.

He lay back down and felt the quiet. "Maybe I should get a cat." Weighing the pros and cons of getting a cat, he turned off the light.

Sometime later he opened his eyes, unable to sleep. After a shot of Benadryl, his "go to" sleeping aid, he closed his eyes to try again. For some reason he started thinking of Raymond. Maybe because he hadn't seen him this week.

A black man in his fifties, Raymond lived in a studio apartment in a downtown Section 8 building. For three years—ever since Jerome had expunged a minor felony from Raymond's record and declined payment—Raymond stopped by his office weekly to say hello. Sheila, the receptionist, per his instructions, never sent him away. "Mr. Konigsberg, Mr. Odems is here to see you."

As Jerome entered the reception area, Raymond—always wearing a multi-color, floppy knit hat—would turn from Sheila: "Mr. Jerome! How you doin' today, Sir?" They would shake hands and talk amicably about the weather or the Cavaliers or the Browns. After five minutes, Raymond would suddenly say, "I thank you, Sir, for your time", shake his hand and exit.

Jerome let it continue because it was only five minutes a week and Raymond never asked for anything. It also seemed to have some kind of meaning for Raymond. Maybe it was hearing the secretary announce him as "Mr. Odems" and then having a well-dressed lawyer come out to shake his hand. As if he was getting something stamped, validation that he had been received at an important place

Jerome switched on a light and reached for a pen on the bedside table. On the back of an envelope he wrote: *Raymond—stamped, validated.* He liked the analogy and wrote more.

If you smile
and say his name
he accepts that in lieu of a passport stamp
If you touch his arm
while smiling and saying his name
he will cup it between his hands and take it home
where, opening his hands to release a butterfly
he proclaims to an empty room
"I exist!"

Pleased, he re-read it. After the last line, something dropped inside himself. He lifted his head and addressed his bedroom doorway and the darkened rooms beyond: "I exist." His voice dissipated at the foot of his bed. "I EXIST!" he shouted. It skipped across the hardwood floor into the house's emptiness until snapped shut in darkness.

Jerome gazed at his uncupped, empty hands. "I really should ....get a cat."

Night Theft

The Black Magus awoke in the night and turned on his bedside light. He groaned upright and reached for the pad and pencil on his nightstand. The dream image—of scaffolding and crumbling buildings—had been exceptionally vivid, as well as the hard-hatted people who lived inside the buildings. He put on his reading glasses and started to write.

We grew too resentful
Constrained by external structures
Dead white men built

Now we are free
To come and go
But never without a hard hat
And safety glasses
Protection
From entire city blocks
of crumbling facades

He re-read it and added a title, Freedom? As he flopped the pad onto the table something fell to the floor. His inhaler? He would have to finish the night propped on his pillows to breathe easier. Satisfied he had deftly captured the dream image, he turned off the light and drew up the covers.

The next morning he awoke, surprised he had slept so well propped up. He remembered why he was in that position. Wincing, he rolled his legs over the edge of the bed, found his glasses, and examined the pad of paper. On it was only one word: Freedom?

He clutched his chin. "I wrote more than one word. Where are they?" He inspected each sheet on the pad, then checked under the covers and behind the pillows. Not finding the missing words he eased himself down the side of the bed onto the carpet. Groaning to his hands and knees he groped for a piece of paper. He felt behind the bedside table and under the bed, found his inhaler, but no verses. "Damn it!"

He sat back against the bed, his fat legs spread apart across the shag carpeting. The door leading to the hallway was all the way open, even though he had, as usual, closed it three quarters before retiring. "I'VE BEEN ROBBED!" he cried.

He reached up for the yellow pad on the bedside table and re-examined it under the lamp light hoping to detect pencil depressions on the blankness below the title, but saw none. In the bottom right hand corner were faintly scribbled pencil markings. He could barely make out what appeared to be two lower-case letters, a "d" and an "a". He glared at the doorway: "d.a.! What is you want from me?!"

Shadows in the hallway flinched, but did not answer. Why would a dead poet steal words from him? And why d.a. levy? He remembered how, yet unpublished, he was intimidated by the slightly older poet's bold precocity, always feeling tongue-tied in his presence. Yet they had been retrospectively twinned as the marquee names of a counter-cultural literary scene to which he had, in reality, been a late arrival. Maybe that was it. Like twins, "his brother's" premature death—barely out of the womb ahead of him—was still exerting invisible waves.

The Black Magus rubbed the back of his neck as if he had been pistol-whipped. *d.a. was always a trickster. Only a trickster would do this.* He started to smile. "At least he didn't take your inhaler, old man." He tilted his head back and raised his arms triumphantly. "I STILL HAVE THOUGHTS WORTH STEALING!"

The dark night would come, he knew, when his new nighttime visitor would peek into his bedroom, sniff, and—detecting nothing of interest—depart, never to return.

Fourth Meeting of the Tenth Triangulum

As Jerome followed Natalija's Corolla down the driveway, he tried to discern her hair profile. Straight back in a bun indicated assertiveness. If loose and stringy—sullenness. If clean and light with sparkling red strands wisping across her face she would be positive, even effusive. Today he sensed a fullness and guessed she would be happier. Although pleased, it also made him—because of something that happened the previous night—concerned.

He dreamt he was crossing a street at a busy downtown intersection. To his right an older man in a fedora hat and trench coat walked slightly ahead of him. On the man's other side he peripherally sensed an attractive woman. About to step onto the curb, he and the woman spontaneously reached behind the man and held hands. It was so vivid that when he awakened he felt the quiet elation of mutual touch. Lying in bed, prolonging the feeling, he whispered a name: "Natalija".

Exiting his car, he assured himself the woman in the dream was better looking than Natalija. But when she stepped out of her car and her clean coppery hair flashed in morning sunlight, he knew it was her hand he had held in his dream.

"Hello," she said, her green eyes smiling in filtered sunlight.

"Your hair looks nice."

"I like your coat."

"A bit brisk today." He looked around. "It's starting to smell like Fall." They gazed up at the maple tree, its red-tinged crown hyper-imposed against blue sky.

"In a few weeks it will be naked," Natalija pronounced.

"Pardon?"

"The tree will be naked."

"Y-yes," he stammered. "Quite so."

"For the Book of Lightness," the Black Magus announced as soon as his pupils were seated, "I would like to suggest a different approach." Sunlight streamed from the kitchen, warming the thin green carpet. The Black Magus seemed unusually relaxed to Natalija. *Something good has happened to him.*

"After reading one of our writings" he continued, "choose the single line that most affects you."

"I'll go," Jerome said. Natalija stretched out a slender hand to receive his writing. Their fingers briefly touched.

"Thank you," she said.

"You're welcome," Jerome said, avoiding eye contact. He started to silently peruse his writing, forgetting to hand a copy to the Black Magus, until the large man cleared his throat.

Recess

I am released with my co-workers
into a large, safe enclosure

Hesitation
then someone starts running
and yelling

We joyfully follow, everyone's
mouth making the same strange noise
racing around a looping walkway
as if giddily chased by a Pamplona bull

Shrubs are bruised
flowers trampled

But then, a cry

Has someone fallen?
Perhaps there are doubts about a bull
We stop running

I double over
throat aching

Around me everyone is panting
or coughing up deep sputum.

Without being told
we file back to the door

Natalija tapped the sheet. "I really like this." Jerome re-read his writing trying to guess what she liked about it. He had been concerned, when composing it, that he was co-opting some of her lilt. Natalija continued. "There should be a holiday when every office worker in Cleveland shows up at Public Square wearing a red sash, ready to run."

The Black Magus perused Jerome over his reading glasses. "So, in seeking lightness we are doomed to fail. We have become irrevocably heavy."

Jerome crossed his legs and leaned back. "I don't mean that every corporate headquarters should be turned into a Chuck E. Cheese, like at Netflix. The older lawyers I work with remember office Christmas parties where the senior partners stripped to their undershirts to arm wrestle. Who plays like *that* anymore?"

The Black Magus nodded then asked Natalija which line struck her most. "I like that everyone is making the same noise, and can't stop. I want to make that noise." She smiled at Jerome, looping hair behind the ear closest to him, exposing her slender neck.

"The line which struck me…." the Black Magus pondered, 'Coughing up a deep sputum.' On the surface it admits defeat. Yet weak infected cells are being expurgated. There is optimism in that."

Jerome nodded, trying not to show surprise. Few people had ever accused him of optimism. He glanced at Natalija. Was her "glimmer" rubbing off on him?

The Black Magus distributed his writing to their outstretched hands.

Cartharsis

My ideal vacation:
For three weeks I am seriously ill

During the first week, a delicious delirium
Transports me to places I have never seen

Halfway through the second week,
still sight-seeing,
But a new sensation:
   The soft vibration of female voices
A hand daubs my forehead
Another puts wetness to my lips

The third week is spent returning
When I am told, "We were worried"
I know I have been
On a daring adventure

Returning to duty
I lift my desk above my head

Natalija spoke first. "'Someone gently daubs my forehead'".

"Another puts wetness to my lips", Jerome added.

The Black Magus frowned. "What about the second stanza?

They quietly re-read it. Jerome held out a half-unfurled hand, palm up. Realizing it was Natalija' gesture he quickly retracted. "So by medically reducing the intensity of illness we deprive our minds of therapeutic wanderings?"

"Yes." the Black Magus replied.

"Delirium," Natalija added, "can be a natural hallucinogen."

"Yes, yes!" the Black Magus cried. "A natural hallucinogen." He wrote it down.

Natalija twisted her mouth. "The biggest takeaway line for me is still that someone lifted your head. You sensed someone was caring for you. Cared about you. Otherwise, why return?"

"Why are you saying 'you'?" The Black Magus snapped.

"Are you writing about someone else?"

The Black Magus nervously tapped his pencil on his notebook. Jerome gazed sideways at Natalija, admiring her directness. And her shiny hair. The Black Magus, scowling and squinting, jotted notes. After a minute he turned to Natalija.

"The Book of Lightness—what do you bring?"

Natalija sucked in her lips and gazed at a spot on the floor, apparently not ready to let the Blake Magus off the hook. Relenting, she leaned forward out of her chair to give the Black Magus a copy of her writing. Jerome detecting a rare opportunity, glanced at her jean-tight buttocks. When she turned to hand him a copy of her writing he recklessly reached and scrunched the paper. "Sorry."

Feast Days

How to shed weight?
Not pounds from my waist,
but from tonnage I drag
in a long bag behind me

Shaking things out doesn't work:
Sisyphus-like, the bag re-fills

Psychologists hire out as Bag Managers
But I would rather try this:

For a whole day
a dozen times a year
I want to drop my bag
and dance with the townspeople,
in the streets, over curbs, in front yards
or on a bridge (like the one at Avignon!)

I want to trip over abandoned bags
and laugh hysterically on the ground

The next day
I find my weight where I left it
After a reluctant hoist
I begin humming a song I learned
the day before

Jerome spoke first. "'dance with the townspeople'".

The Black Magus followed: "'I begin humming a song I learned the day before'."

Jerome pivoted to Natalija. "Townspeople have been relegated to fairy tales. Your writing makes me want to have townspeople in my life." Natalija beamed.

The Black Magus jotted notes, reviewed them, then breathed nasally, building to a pronouncement. "We have forgotten how to run and yell together; bringing up sputum is a symptom of this, but also a catharsis. We have vanquished the sick bed where we can travel to faraway places and where loved ones apply moisture to bring us back. We have forgotten how to dance in the streets or laugh on the ground. We no longer sing together to help carry our burdens."

Natalija sighed. "We have forgotten how to be light."

The Black Magus held up a finger. "But today we are remembering. Nicely done!" Jerome and Natalija straightened at the rare kudos. The Black Magus cleared his throat and smacked the arm of his chair. "Let us look at some of the other lines. There is much worth noting."

After Jerome and Natalija exited, the Black Magus watched as they chatted between their cars. He could tell the lawyer was the one who delayed leaving. She was harder to read—allowing glimpses, but then self-sealing. He glazed into a stare soon eclipsed by a familiar image: himself lying in his bed looking sickly, his face thinner, beard grayer. A slender hand extended and daubed perspiration from his forehead. It was Natalija's. She appeared several years older but with a serene beauty. Was she there as a former pupil out of charity? Or professionally, as a nurse with Hospice Care? Or, was she there in a more intimate role?

He sighed. "Yes, yes. It would have been nice......to have a daughter."

He watched their cars disappear down the drive. Usually this was a satisfying moment—a welcome return to quiet after intense people exposure. Now, he gazed sadly at the changing trees. The leaves would be gone in another month. Thereafter, young writers would no longer come to his house.

Chapter 7

The Book of Waking Up

Cloudlight

The dinner trays had been collected and calm pervaded the nursing facility. When it was nice outside, Natalija usually took one or two women out for a walk or to sit on a bench. But this evening all her ladies politely declined, perhaps resting for Bingo.

She strolled through the facility's square layout alone in the hallway, the low voices of visitors or tv commercials seeping from rooms. Halfway around she encountered the new director of nursing, Sheila Gray, visiting from the other building.

"Well, Natty, I guess I missed dinner," Sheila said.

"I can have the kitchen put something together for you," Natalija offered.

"No, no. I'm fine." Sheila crossed her arms then tapped Natalija on the wrist. "Question. Have you thought about getting a degree?" Natalija froze. She had been researching writing programs at local colleges with a view toward teaching. "I've heard so many good things about you," Sheila continued. "You could do so much more as a nurse if you had a B.S."

Natalija crossed her arms and slowly nodded. "If I was an RN, I wouldn't get to spend as much time with my ladies." Her ladies had helped save her. She loved them, and the thought of spending more time on administrative duties, despite higher pay and prestige, made her uneasy.

"An admirable quality," Sheila said. "But give it some thought. I'm on the board at Ursuline and there are scholarships to be had." Sheila commenced talking about the merits of the Ursuline School of Nursing's weekend program. Over Sheila's right shoulder, Natalija noticed an orange glow down the hallway, entering from the right. After eight years she knew the seasonal patterns of sunlight in this hallway. This time of day, this time of year, that side of the building should be in shadow.

Sheila's intense eye contact made it difficult for her to observe the mysterious glow. When a resident tottered past and Sheila turned to say hello, Natalija stole a look. The glow was bulging in from the right. And strengthening. For a chilling second she thought it might be a fire. But it was too even. Too steady.

Sheila seemed to notice she was distracted. "I'm sorry—you have things to do. But please, consider Ursuline. I can help."

They walked in opposite directions, Natalija toward the orange glow. It emanated through sliding glass doors which led to a small red brick patio, its furniture recently removed to winter storage. She slid open the glass door and stepped out.

A solitary cloud, sculpted against blue sky, hovered over the one-story facility like a gigantic hot air balloon. Drinking in orange from the setting sun, the weight of color spilled downward. Natalija walked to the center of the patio. The thick draping orange coated her eyelids and fused her legs to the red brick pavers. Realizing she was basking in cloud light—a first—she pushed up her sleeves and opened her hands.

Over the next few minutes the cloud nudged east until stalling over an adjacent field. Natalija placed her hands on her hips like a scolding mother. "If I offer you something, you might stay, and you can't!"

After a minute her new cloud-friend resumed its migration, its sides denting purple from the rapidly setting sun behind her. A few fields away, grey strands of rain unfurled from its underside.

"Moist tentacles," Natalija whispered, "brushing a few acres of earth".

Behind her the sun slipped behind a line of trees and the patio instantly cooled. The solitary cloud accelerated, becoming a darkening mountain. Natalija started to wave good-bye, but a childhood memory stopped her arm: a stray dog she had petted and almost named, trotting into the dusk.

Backyard Experiment

Jerome was aware that within the Triangulum he was the most literal. Although he felt his writings carved solid images and dared to say something, he sensed he couldn't make the gravity-defying poetic leaps the other two could. Compared to Natalija, who was lighter on her feet with words, he felt he was wearing heavy boots, trudging out each line. A recent exchange with the Black Magus still rankled.

"You tend to be coiled up in your head."

"Are you saying I need more heart?"

"More stomach and intestines. And lower."

At first he let the observation glance off, as he had the pronouncements of the three psychiatrists he had visited over the last year. When each of them asked about his upbringing he delivered the same encapsulation. "Nothing major. My father was an architect. We kept out of each other's way for the most part but seemed to get along. Our best moments were colluding around my mother, trying to keep her from going off. She has a super high I.Q. and was probably never happy because of that. She buzzed through law school in two years in her late 30s, worked for the ACLU for 15 years, then headed a Jewish non-profit that gives no-interest loans to low-income college students. My parents divorced five years ago and live ten miles apart in St. Petersburg, near my sister's family. I go down once a year. It's always a little weird, but okay. My father is thinking of re-marrying but....yeah, it's all good."

By the third therapist—a woman this time to see if that made a difference— he had edited out "a little weird, but okay" since it seemed to attract the most attention. In analyzing why he never made it to a third session with any of the therapists, he isolated two conflicting reasons: 1) it seemed to be going nowhere fast, or 2) a lid was about to come off, and he wasn't sure he wanted it to. He felt he was approaching that same critical juncture with the "Triangulum/Fellowship", a sarcastic term he had tried out on Natalija without the intended result, probably because he failed to say it sarcastically.

On Sunday morning, coffee mug in hand, he sat down in his grandfather's high-backed, upholstered chair and surveyed his empty living room. "Too coiled up in my head, am I?" He thought hard about it and, after three cups of coffee, distilled a concept: experiential. He had never liked the word and sensed he had chosen law because it entailed never having to attend an "experiential workshop". But did his aversion to such things hint at a missing piece?

"Why not?" he asked the living room. This week he needed to bring a writing for *The Book of Waking Up*. Why not attempt a new composing process, less cerebral and more experiential?

He would write about waking up in an unusual place and—to leverage his senses rather than his pre-frontal cortex—actually put his body in that place. Maybe that would uncoil him from his brain.

At 10:45pm he stepped off his patio deck and, carrying a new sleeping bag, two pillows, a water bottle, Benadryl, and flashlight, tip-toed into his backyard. It would be the best "weather night" this week: dry and unseasonably warm. Earlier he had prepared a spot, laying down a top-of-the-line inflatable camping pad under the sheltering canopy of a mature Red Maple. The tree's wide trunk and shrubs shielded him from the Josephs, his early-rising neighbors to the right. Although the Simons, a retired couple on the other side, were out of town, he aligned three patio chairs on that side to create a comforting barrier.

Before climbing into the sleeping bag he draped a power cord over a chair and plugged in a small audio device that claimed to deter small animals and, he hoped, medium size ones. Although too cool for mosquitos, he wasn't so sure about spiders and sprayed insect repellant around the sleeping bag's perimeter to create a chemical moat. He climbed into the bag and next to his head he arranged the water bottle, his phone, and Benadryl.

Lying on his back, he stared into the dark branches of the maple above. A faint breeze tickled his face, drying his eyeballs. He listened to solitary cars on nearby streets and watched light from the Joseph's 90 inch flat screen strobe against the tree trunk. *What if I can't fall asleep?* He thought of the unopened bottle of Xanax in his bathroom cabinet and how that might help. Prescribed by the female psychiatrist for *Anxiety Disorder –Unspecified*, he had dutifully filled the prescription. Not entirely sold on the diagnosis, he consigned the pills as an auxiliary medical supply. But the full bottle sometimes made him nervous. Like having a loaded gun in the house.

Around 11:20pm the Joseph's house lights dimmed. A few stars glinted through the branches and the anti-rodent device crackled faintly, like a Geiger counter. "Damn it!" He propped himself on an elbow and reached for the Benadryl. To expedite unconsciousness, he poured himself a double dose.

Orion

The Black Magus felt the past week had been his most productive in years. Three new writings!

Something was building beneath the over-machined green lawns and he was relieved he still had it in him to react, relieved that his warrior loins had not permanently cooled. "Potency!" he shouted, raising a triumphant fist.

Certainly Orion had helped. For countless winters he had gazed out his back window at the night sky, beseeching the great hunter for a pinch of his hunter-warrior energy. Recently reappearing in the autumn skies, had Orion finally heard him?

Coining the three writings "The Orion Trilogy", he was eager to showcase them to his two pupils. He rehearsed his presentation speech: "Old warriors are dying and new warriors must be trained. You have earned this honor. These writings are not for any Book. They are for you: the gift of fierceness." He re-read them, imagining his pupils reading them for the first time.

Commencement

Above you the tree branch
Where they hung your umbilical cord to dry
Can you see it, now withered and hard?

Its nourishment is gone
Even crows no longer regard it as suet

It is time to take it down

Rite of Passage

Before dawn,
Paint your body blue
Take up a spear
Follow the other painted bodies
out from the village

In ground darkness, the
Small herd of pre-dawn men
Moves through a night-dampened field
Wet grasses tugging bare legs

How is it you are part of this?
If you tell them you forgot something
They will not stop and wait

When the sun rises
Blue skin gleams all around you
You are among warriors

At such a fine moment
You finally stop wondering
Why you left your mother's womb

Grey Warrior

Would you be a grey warrior?
A watcher of the night
Blazing trails through morning dew
Juking the mid-day glare
A friend to the first darkness
Which gathers under trees

He looked forward to presenting the new writings to his two pupils. They knew his weekly contributions to each Book were mainly re-workings—a word here, a phrase there—of compositions tested throughout previous Triangula. How nice it would be to announce: "Behold! The Orion Series!"

But he was still unsure of one phrase in *Rite of Passage*: "pre-dawn men". Women needed to be among the new warriors. Indeed, between his two pupils the female was the fiercer. He tried replacing it with "pre-dawn people" and then "pre-dawn men and women", and even "pre-dawn folk". But none seemed right. There was also another problem: if the pre-dawn group was of both genders, so much skin showing at sunrise, even if painted, might cause a different reaction.

Doubts about the entire trilogy soon intruded. Was the true motive for presenting these new writings to help his pupils gird for when the surface finally broke? Or was it vainly meant to demonstrate that, creatively, he was far from impotent?

Rinsing his coffee cup, his excitement about The Orion Trilogy eroded. The writings spoke urgently to an alarming need. But he knew the writings lacked authenticity.

"How long, fat man," he asked himself, "since you carved a path through the morning dew? Have you taken down your own over-pecked unbiblical cord, or is it still blackening? When, pray tell, did you carry a spear with other men?"

He gazed sadly through the kitchen window at the pear tree in the corner of his neighbor's back yard, its branches bent low with fruit. A long dormant voice trumpeted inside his head. *YOU ARE STILL A WARRIOR! RUN OUT THE BACK DOOR AND STEAL A PEAR. NOW!*

Fifth Meeting of the Tenth Triangulum

Jerome arrived at 9:54 and parked. He calculated that this was the fifth book which meant he would be coming here five more times. While he waited for Natalija he checked work emails. At 9:59 he placed his phone on the console and got out. With no sign of his fellow pupil's red Corolla, he would have to enter the Black Magus' house alone.

His host greeted him with a nod, looking past him for Natalija. Jerome instantly noticed the teacher had gotten a haircut, a conspicuously uneven one. Knowing there was little chance for poly-syllabic small talk he generated his own. *Nice haircut. Who's your stylist? Just a wild guess, but is it Tony?*

They waited silently for Natalija. The Black Magus seemed unusually static, not making the eccentric nasal sounds which usually preceded sessions. Jerome checked the wall clock: 10:02. Until they were "three" the Black Magus would be dysfunctional. The small floor fan in the corner was turned off and the silence finally forced him to speak.

"What was d.a. levy like?"

The Black Magus' twitched, then glared at him. "That's the second time you've asked me about him. Why?"

"No reason. Curious."

The large man's glare softened into a gaze, looking deeper into Jerome. "You've thought about it, haven't you?"

"Thought about what?"

"The act d.a. committed on himself at age 26. For yourself."

Jerome nervously re-crossed his legs. "That was a bit of a leap!" Phil Lundy's eerie description echoed: *A bullet to the third eye in the lotus position.*

The Black Magus continued to gaze at him. "d.a. has been in my dreams of late." His eyes glimmered sadly. "Maybe I am coming full circle. Back to the place before my beginning. Maybe that's why my appointed womb-brother has come back to taunt me. The serpent's head is curling back to swallow its tail."

Jerome angled his head, mimicking Natalija's radar dish reaction to the Black Magus' more abstruse remarks. Light reflecting off a car flashed across the walls. *She's here.* Outside, a car door slammed and a moment later the front door opened.

"Traffic," Natalija chirped. "Sorry." Her hair sported a new category: damp. Jerome wondered which Natalija it portended. Perhaps because of her lateness, the Black Magus inflicted prolonged nostril expansions and contractions upon them. After a minute he addressed Natalija.

"What do you bring—four minutes late—to *The Book of Waking Up?*"

Natalija hooked her wet hair over her right ear leaving her slender fingers delicately bent in the air. Jerome jotted on the inside of his folder: *expressive fingers, pausing in air, half-uncurled, moist from wet hair.*

Unperturbed by the teacher's scolding, Natalija handed out her writing and they bowed their heads to read.

Snapping Through

Trying to fight through the
heavy shrink wrap entombing me

Arms pinned to sides
forehead clamped

What is this pocket I can't get out of?

My packaged existence vacillates between cozy,
and a fear of un-germed sterility

I push out my arms

one breaks free

then the other

Straining forward
I snap through, tumbling
into jarring street noise
and sudden stares

My eyes are already smarting,
Heart pounding

Brushing off the plastic tatters of my shroud
I shoulder my way in

"You've captured my morning commute," Jerome joked. Natalija didn't smile. He re-scanned her writing, scrambling to make amends with a serious compliment.

The Black Magus peered over his reading glasses. "Men who survive big cat attacks recall a zen-like acceptance at being snugly clamped in the jaws of something inescapably powerful. Plastic shroud layers are also jaws."

Natalija tilted her head, unspooling his remarks. The Black Magus continued. "Your writing starts with a prisoner and ends with a warrior. When we act, it is the warrior who shakes us. " His right hand started to open and close as if gripping something. "Yes, there is a young warrior in this room."

Jerome bit his lower lip. The teacher had a way of building up with one hand and knocking down with the other. Even though it wasn't yet his turn, he already felt knocked down. After bestowing Natalija's writing with a few more compliments, the Black Magus handed out copies of his own writing. "What I bring".

The Re-Moistening

Skulls bleaching salt white
Everything flattening into desert

From the Divine Medicine Dropper
I crave
Just one drop of water
To smack down atop my cranium
Roll coldly down the back of my head
—vaporizing on my burning neck

Send a shiver back through me!

Startle me awake!

Natalija, hunching over her crossed legs, turned quizzically to the Black Magus. "Divine Medicine Dropper is capitalized. Do you mean God?"

The Black Magus squinted at the lines.

"The water" Jerome said, attempting to moderate, "is coming from above and—coming from a medicine dropper—is intended to heal. I interpret that line as 'healing water from above.'"

"How is that not God?" Natalija asked, unfurling fingers. She leaned out over her crossed-legs toward the Black Magus. "Is it God you crave?"

The Black Magus held up an index finger. "All I am asking for is one drop."

Natalija clutched her damp hair behind her head. "But WHOM are you asking? If you are waiting for something then it must be coming from somewhere, and you must believe it exists."

"But does something exist," Jerome countered, "if it never arrives?"

The Black Magus re-read his writing, then removed his reading glasses. "Natalija is correct. My writing is more about waiting than waking. It may not be appropriate for this Book."

Natalija's jaw dropped. "I didn't mean….."

The Black Magus held up a hand to quiet her then looked down to jot notes with the other hand. Finished writing, the Black Magus lowered his raised arm and turned to Jerome. "What do you bring to The Book of Waking Up?"

Jerome wanted to prep them by explaining his new experiential approach to writing, but knowing the Black Magus would stop him, handed out his writing.

Bacchus Was Here

Blinking dew from my eyelids
I remember I am lying on my back
under a tree
in somebody's backyard

Staring straight up, a transformation:
First sunlight paints branches orange

The tiny movements of a sparrow amaze me

How have I never seen this?

Men and women in summer clothing
lie strewn across the lawn, no
two of them pointed the same way,
like the hundreds of empty
green or brown bottles resting between them

In the yellowing light, it is
calming to watch chests rise and fall
Upturned faces tilt to one side
as if towards a loved one

I don't remember their names
It is enough that we slept and will awaken
in the same backyard

I stand up, unusually refreshed
There is no need to disturb my new friends

I will let myself out at the gate.

They read and re-read it quietly. Jerome realized he had mentioned a gate but no fence. The writing had incubated only a few short days and other things about it started to look wrong to him.

The Black Magus pointed at a line. "I have a question about—"

Natalija interrupted. "'In the yellowing light, it is calming to watch chests rise and fall.' That is so beautiful."

Jerome gazed at her. Her slender fingers, peeking through the loose sleeve of her white sweater, held his writing. He felt a sudden desire to crumple forward onto one knee and bury his eyes in her soft sweater. She turned to the Black Magus. "I'm sorry. I cut you off."

The Black Magus resumed. "You mention a gate. Which implies a fence, a barrier."

Jerome smiled. "A low picket fence, actually."

"Yes," the Black Magus replied, "that is what I saw." He removed his glasses. "I am in agreement with my colleague." He gestured toward Natalija. "She used the word 'beautiful'. I would say 'sublime' is more accurate. Sublimity always involves a crossing over. There are several crossings in your writing. The last, and most important, will occur after the gate opens and closes."

Jerome gazed at the heavyset, goateed man in a blue workman's shirt. He felt an overpowering urge to lurch forward onto one knee, grasp the older man's hand, and place it atop his bowed head.

Chapter 8

The Book of Hypermodernity

The Literary League

Jerome, realizing he was spending too many evenings at home by himself, decided to place himself in a challenging public situation.

After parking at a meter, he walked down Coventry's main business drag past its old storefronts. He had not attended a Literary League poetry reading for several months and felt that—since he was currently benefitting from one of their fellowships—he should be more supportive.

He found the alley for Mac's Back's Books and entered its coolness. A green haired young man preceded him and he feared he would be the eldest. He entered the used bookstore's worn book cover smells, soothingly non-digital. A handsome, sixtyish-looking woman shelving books smiled at him. He was sure her name was Suzanne but, playing it safe, he silently returned her smile and wended his way to a back room, relieved to hear voices. *I won't be the only one.*

About twenty people milled about, some already seating themselves. He recognized a pudgy older man with a visored captain's hat. *The tricycle poet.* The last time he heard him read he started by performing comical figure 8s on a large trike before stopping to face the audience. After a few tricycle jokes he read heart-rending poems about his lifelong struggle with mental illness. Although glad to see someone older, Jerome was relieved to not see a tricycle.

Not an evening coffee drinker, Jerome nevertheless poured some from a white carafe into a small Styrofoam cup, sprinkled in some non-dairy creamer and, unable to find a stir stick, sloshed it around, at the same time scouting the seating. Thirty or so folding metal chairs were arranged into four rows. He grabbed a copy of the League's latest newsletter and took an outside seat in the third row on the less populated left-hand side.

After browsing the newsletter he perused the room. A woman in her late 40s with grey streaked black hair had taken a seat a few rows ahead on the opposite side. She looked familiar. *Medical. Where? What was that shrink's name? Barlow. His receptionist!* Dr. Barlow had been one of his most recent therapy attempts. After two sessions, the doctor diagnosed *Depressive Disorder – Undifferentiated* and had prescribed Zoloft. After taking the anti-depressant for six weeks he stopped. Although it seemed to blunt the lows, there was an unacceptable side effect: he had stopping dreaming at night. Or stopped remembering dreams. Since then, the pills had been relegated to his scrap bin of auxiliary medical supplies.

The receptionist, overdressed with a colorful scarf and white pants, gazed to her left toward a front corner of the room past a solitary chair set up for the readers. Something about the look made Jerome take notice: she wasn't so much staring at something—since there was nothing in the corner—but *into* something. He remembered lines from *The Opening*, the poem the Black Magus had mailed him after their first meeting.

Train your eyes/To look for The Opening. Was this woman inadvertently showing "a scratch in her Teflon"?

He politely looked away, then peeked again. She was still gazing into the corner. From the back of the room a familiar male voice called his name. Surprised, he twisted around. Phil Lundy waved him to come over.

Phil, his white mane academically draped behind him, smiled through his thick black glass frames. "Jerome, I'd like you to meet Hank Tanaka." An Asian-American man near in age to Jerome smilingly offered his hand. "Hank," Phil continued, "was a fellowship recipient three…four years ago?"

"Yes", Hank answered. He turned to Jerome. "How are things going?"

For a moment Jerome wasn't sure what they were talking about. "Oh, the fellowship. Its….been interesting."

"Excuse me," Phil said, checking his watch. "I need to get this thing going." He left them to make his way toward the front.

Hank smiled. "I've heard you are the last?"

"The last Triangulum? We are, me and Natalija…." He could not remember her last name and looked around the room as if she might be there to prompt him. "She's the other 'pupil'". Hank smiled at the reference. Phil was motioning people to sit; Jerome realized he only had time to ask a quick question. "Do you still keep in touch with…the teacher?"

Hank turned his head away and smiled wryly. "Yes, and no."

"How so?"

He turned back to Jerome and eyed him curiously. "You haven't gotten to The Clearing yet."

Jerome remembered it as the Tenth Book. "We're on the eighth book. Hypermodernity." Hank nodded. "We should get together," Jerome suggested. "It would be interesting to exchange notes. With a Triangulum Project alumnus."

Hank smiled. "I'd be happy to."

"I'll get your number after the reading."

Jerome started toward his seat thinking Hank might follow and sit near him, but Hank walked to the other side and sat next to a good-looking black man he seemed to know.

Phil launched into introductory remarks. Jerome wondered if Phil might acknowledge him—*I'm pleased to see that one of this year's fellowship winners, Jerome Konigsberg, is here this evening. Jerome, can you give us a wave?*—but it didn't happen. The first poet to read was a young man in a suit jacket and string tie, late twenties, with short blond hair neatly slicked to one side. He confidently hurled into a poem titled *Floating Shards*. Jerome thought the lines had an angular sharpness, certain words pricking the listener's senses. But he couldn't discern the poem's meaning.

The second poet was a young women with a face raw from acne. Her nervousness and quiet voice seemed to draw the audience in, a sharp contrast to the first poet who had jutted out-of-the-frame like a cubist painting. Two lines from her last poem—*Stop pouring yourself / Into the opaque bottle of adulthood*—caught his attention and he regretted not paying more attention to previous lines.

After noting the voice and confidence of each poet in turn, his attention wandered. He felt an unexpected yearning for the Triangulum and their silent readings. He occasionally turned to observe the receptionist. She listened attentively and smiled when she clapped. *Why is she here by herself? Is she here to support someone? Why is she a receptionist?* Her applause—polite, earnest— was equal for all the readers. *What caused her to stare into nothingness?*

He glanced a few rows behind her at Hank Tanaka. Hank's shoulder was comfortably pressed against the black man next to him. He studied Hank's face. *He's been through the Triangulum.*

But how did it change him? He searched Hank's face for some sign of a spiritual superiority. He thought back to the moment before the reading when Hank looked away after he asked him if he kept in touch with the Black Magus. "*Yes, and no*". And then Hank's oblique reference to The Clearing. Why the strange look?

The reading lasted an hour. After Phil thanked everyone for coming, most attendees got up to talk to someone else. He and the receptionist were the only ones unengaged. She slowly adjusted and re-adjusted her scarf, pausing to peruse and re-arrange the literature she had collected. Jerome remembered other lines from The Opening*:*

When you see it, don't be too tired!
Move closer until you feel its breeze

But if he approached her, what would he say? *I couldn't help noticing how, earlier, you were staring into the void. I have glimpsed it too. Do you have time for a coffee?* She stood and put on her jacket. He would have to act fast. Uncertain, he decided to place himself in her way to see if anything would happen.

He casually positioned himself near the doorway and perused his program. When he sensed her approaching he looked up. As she neared, he noticed slight bags under her eyes. At the last second she looked up at him; glistening brown eyes offset the tiredness in her face. She politely smiled with no indication she remembered his two office visits to Dr. Barlow; he reflexively returned the smile. She slipped past him leaving a floral scent in her wake. *She put on a fragrance to come here.*

He had failed to act but had a readymade excuse: he had promised Hank he would get his contact information. Hank and his partner were talking to a young poet who had participated in the reading. The young man patted his chest, pantomiming nervousness. Hank spoke to him reassuringly. After a minute, Hank went over to the soft-spoken young woman with acne. Phil Lundy brushed past Jerome from behind, calling to someone across the room. Jerome moved from the doorway, glancing once more at Hank. *There is nothing exceptional about him.* He rolled up his program and exited.

He entered the darkening alley outside the bookstore. Looking toward the sidewalk ahead he increased his pace then broke into a jog. Emerging onto the street, he shielded his eyes from streetlights and car headlights and scanned the sidewalks for a woman wearing a scarf and white pants. Seeing nothing he searched the other side. She was gone. Jerome, twisting the rolled-up program in both hands, murmured the last stanza of *The Opening*:

Note its location and dimensions
So you can circle back
Knowing full well
It will no longer be there

The Gash

Natalija opened her eyes, surprised to see daylight. The room was unusually still. Had she come upon the room so suddenly that it was unaware of her presence?

The bed sheets contoured her body, resting on her breasts and knees, sinking between her thighs. She waited for something to happen. Would it be an epiphany about life? Or the discovery of some hidden meanings in the room? A moment later a door slammed somewhere in the building and the rare stillness scuttled back into the walls. "Thanks a lot, Keesha," she hissed at her neighbor, whose heels clattered across the parking area outside.

About to get up she remembered something important had happened last night. She propped herself and checked the jotting on her bedside note pad. *Water running down wounded tree.*

She collapsed back onto the pillow. The dream had been extraordinarily vivid. And disturbing! She knew she needed to re-enter it. If she didn't do so now, its imaginal power would atrophy and she would never know what it was trying to tell her. Her heart started to pound. "No, you need to go back. No more backpeddaling!" She closed her eyes, controlled her breathing, and coaxed the images to re-appear.

Re-starting at a distance, the first image was of her simple room in Vuzenica, her bed with the red quilt and the smooth plank floor with the thick throw rug she used to stumble over. But instead of being on the second floor of the house, the room was on the first. The one window, wide open, looked out—not into Aunt Alenka's yard—but into the pub courtyard where they lunched on Sundays. The tables and chairs were gone. In the middle was the tree they sat under, a mature cherry.

Unlike the last time she saw the tree—when they caught its falling blossoms in their wine glasses—it was just starting to bud. Around its ten inch base sunlight glinted on melting snow and quaking puddles. With melt water trickling in the gutters, she climbed through the window and went up to the tree, stepping barefoot through alternately warm and cold puddles. Earth smells and a mild Spring breeze lifted her hair. About three feet up the purplish trunk, water spilled from an ugly gash. She desperately wanted the gushing to stop and looked for a First Aid kit. Seeing none, she knelt to apply direct pressure.

Pressing her right hand over the cut, warm water streamed through her fingers. The harder she pressed the more forcefully it spurted, spraying onto her eyes. Suddenly, another hand, large and tanned, clamped over hers. "Hey!" she cried, annoyed at the intrusion. But despite pressing hard against her hand, it did not hurt. The water stopped spurting. *Is it Him?* She looked for a nail wound in the middle of the hand, but the hand suddenly withdrew and the water again hemorrhaged through her fingers. She clamped her left hand over her right and squeezed her eyes shut. "STOP!" About to scream, she realized something had changed. Slowly withdrawing her hand, the wound, no longer streaming water, revealed itself, an irregular gash, as if from a vicious axe swing. She pressed the back of two fingers against the trunk below the gash and the water dribbled over them, reduced to a trickle.

She opened her eyes. Sunlight streamed in around the window shade. "It's slowing!" she exclaimed to the room. "It's slowing!"

Museum

The Black Magus sat in his window-facing chair trying to bend a negative into a positive.

Slept poorly last night
But at least it means I won't die today:
I am simply too tired to travel anywhere far

He re-read the freshly penned lines and waited to feel better, but it didn't happen. He attributed this latest bout of insomnia to a growing affliction which needed to be addressed. "Today!" he yelled at the window.

Since the affliction affected motor control in his hand, he wondered if it was neurological. But a more tantalizing theory kept surfacing: an ancient memory was erupting. The only way to confirm was to conduct field research. He went to the wall phone in the kitchen and dialed Tony. "Can you take me to the Art Museum?"

"You actually want to go someplace?"

"Well?"

"Give me an hour."

As they cruised Fairmount Boulevard, sunlight twinkled through leafy trees. It was an unusually warm October day and, at the Black Magus' request, Tony lowered the windows. Tony's long hair lifted as it had the day he first got his license, when they had driven down this same street, through the same filtered light in Tony's Ford Fairlane. Even in high school he knew he and Tony, unlike their classmates, were destined for wayward pathways. Like himself, although more pragmatically, Tony lived in the gaps between how other people lived.

After a 16-month tour in Viet Nam chauffeuring army brass—and sometimes their Vietnamese mistresses—around Saigon, Tony came home and became a valet parking attendant at an east side country club, rapidly rising to parking manager. To supplement his income he developed a select customer list among club members. While they dined or golfed, he duck-taped packets of white powder under their dashboards. His tips were in hundred dollar bills. That ended twenty years later when—with declining membership in the 1990s—new board members questioned why a full-time parking manager with benefits was needed. Tony, ever resourceful, transitioned to ticket brokering for sports and concert events, later adding baseball cards. He even had a website.

The Black Magus, remembering how on that first drive together they stopped at a drug store to buy cigarettes, pointed ahead. "A drug store is coming up. I think it's now a CVS. Do you need smokes?"

"Smokes? Haven't heard that one for a while."

In the CVS parking lot, the Black Magus remained in the car. A young woman with long brown hair passed within inches of his open window, skin-tight pants displaying every contour of her curvy buttocks, accentuated by a sensuous twitch. In her wake, a flowery scent. The Black Magus could not divert his eyes from her perfection. When she disappeared into the store, he retrieved a small notepad from his shirt pocket and started writing.

To be touched once more....by the goddess.

He gazed at the store entrance, feeling a disturbing impulse to get out of the car and follow her down the aisles. He resumed writing.

Which is why I would build a temple
To someone I've only glimpsed
From behind.

The other door opened and Tony hopped in. The Black Magus looked wistfully at the store entrance. "Did you need somethin'?" Tony asked. "You shoulda said."

The Black Magus jammed the notepad into his shirt pocket. "Something to build a temple with."

"You wanna go to Home Depot?"

The Black Magus clapped sharply. "To the Art Museum!"

The Museum had completed a major renovation since he had last visited in the 90s and the Black Magus was unsure where to go. He approached the nearest guard. "The Armor Court? Please tell me it survived this slickness."

"Second floor, old building," the guard said, pointing the way.

After several minutes they entered a large sky-lit room with marble-paneled walls. In the center majestically stood a knight in full armor on an equally armored horse.

"On school field trips I used to really dig that dude!" Tony crowed.

The Black Magus scanned the displays of gleaming weaponry, then hobbled toward a long, tall glass case along the rear wall. He shuffled sideways until stopping in front of three broadswords, vertically arrayed in ascending height. The blades of the two on the left were pewter grey. The third and largest sword was less tarnished. All three retained their beaded grips. The Black Magus's eyes darted from one to the other

Tony came alongside. "What's goin' on with your hand? Looks like you're squeezin' a stress ball."

The Black Magus, leaning on his cane with his left hand, examined his right hand which kept opening and closing. "Tony, can hands have ancient memories?"

Tony extended an arm and closed his fingers around an invisible handle. "Mine is remembering a flagon of ale."

"Okay, Falstaff," the Black Magus groused. He reached toward the sword on the far left, his hand corkscrewing downward until it bumped against the glass. "Medieval burial sites of high-status warriors often reveal swords broken into several pieces, ritually disabled to ensure there was no coming back for the deceased. Just think of all the broken warrior energy moldering underground. But what if an intact ancient sword was 're-united' with a modern warrior's hand? Would it bring back the deep light?"

Tony leaned forward. "You like that one?" He pointed at the shortest, dullest sword on the left. "The other two are in better shape."

"It is the oldest." For the second time that day he felt a disturbing desire, this time to smash open a glass display case with his cane. "It's like I am ten years old again, salivating outside the plate glass window at Hough Bakery." He stepped back. "I am unquenched. But at least I know."

"Know what?

"The object of my thirst."

Tony held out a closed hand and let go of his invisible flagon. "To unquenched hands! Hey, ya think you can handle some lunch?"

Sixth Meeting of the Tenth Triangulum

When Natalija arrived for the next meeting there was an older model gold Cadillac parked in the Black Magus' driveway. It bothered her. Over the course of the past week, she had envisioned driving down the puddled driveway and smiling as the flaking white house came into view. The Cadillac had not been part of that image.

As she stood next to her car, a buzzing noise worked its way around the rear corner of the house. Tony, his silver locks dangling under his Cleveland Indians hat, came into view trimming overgrown grass near the foundation. At the front corner he shut off the grass trimmer and ambled over.

"Top of the mornin' to ya". A small gold ear cuff glinted under his hat.

"It is a nice morning." They watched a yellow leaf sail past and land on the hood of her car. Natalija motioned toward the unkempt house. The tiny leaves on the still growing maple seedlings in the front gutter were coloring red. "Is there anything we can do to help?"

Tony leaned on the weed whacker in a jaunty frontiersman pose, elbows out. "He's never liked the manicured look. 'Over-machined' he calls it."

"How long has he lived here?"

"They moved in about 25 years ago."

"They?"

"He and his dad. Mr. C. passed in '99."

"Were they close?"

Tony gazed furtively at the house and chuckled. "Carstairs and Hop 'n Poop."

"Sorry?"

"Mr. C's daily poison—bottom shelf whisky on the rocks, with two packets of Sweet 'n Low." Natalija grimaced. Tony re-adjusted his stance. "They used to have a nice house in Cleveland Heights."

"What happened?"

"Mr. C. was a high-powered salesman back in the day. But he drank himself into a new job every two or three years, each one less pay. They downsized through eight places before they landed here. When he retired, he was hawking T-shirts at the minor league park".

Natalija followed Tony's gaze to the house. Tony massaged the back of his neck. "Every summer Bear got his shrink to admit him into a mental hospital for two weeks so he and his pop could take a vacation from each other. But you know what? His old man visited him every day. Go figure."

A sparrow fluttered between them. Tony held out an index finger and the sparrow alighted. After jerking its head about—seeming to check them out—it hopped atop Tony's hat, then fluttered away.

"Oh my God!" Natalija gasped. "Does that happen often?"

"What, the bird?" Tony thought about it. "A couple of times."

They searched the trees for other magical birds. "What about his mother?" Natalija asked.

"He was in his twenties when she passed. Cancer. Great lady. Very Irish Catholic."

"He's Catholic?"

Tony wobbled his head. "The only time he asks me to take him to mass is on her birthday. And on The Assumption."

They quietly watched another yellow leaf sa shay past. "No other family?" Natalija asked.

"A sister in Arizona. Rachel hasn't been back since Mr. C died. They talk a couple times a year."

From behind, a car crackled down the drive, Jerome's Audi. Natalija touched Tony's forearm. "Its great that he has you."

Tony winked. "We got each other's backs."

As Natalija and Jerome entered the house, they stopped talking and dutifully took their seats, triangulated with the teacher's. After checking the wall clock, the Black Magus set his elbows on the chair arms and brought his fingertips together.

"Today we bring to the sixth book—*The Book of Hyper-Modernity*." He put on his reading glasses, then extended a hand which he moved around as if checking the atmospheric conditions inside the triangle. "Instead of reading one writing at a time, we shall read three simultaneously. Pass your writing to the person on your right. When you are done reading, pass again, until we have passed three times."

Jerome and Natalija worked it out in their heads, then passed their writing to the person on their right. "Wait!" The Black Magus said. "Reverse that."

They changed directions, Natalija receiving Jerome's writing.

Digital Death Camp

Please do not show me THE PICTURES
the squibbed humanoid lines, Matisse-like
of your child-to-be

I am glad your fetus is healthy
but why ruin its pre-wakefulness?
Let it sleep longer
un-poked by Doppler

Then again, perhaps it is best to
condition your not-yet-born
to the digitalization of its life
Honor it as the first screen image
of the five hundred thousand to follow

To absorb so many images
they must be de-powered

Each can live for only a moment
before sentenced to digital storage in
overcrowded image death camps, four to a bunk
eventually becoming body stacks
only a bulldozer can move

Natalija jotted her first thought: *He wants to have children and is bitter it might not happen.* Knowing she was projecting a personal concern, she crossed out what she had just written.

The Black Magus had received Natalija's verses.

Lost Art

No one stares at my face
intrigued by what it might say about me

There were once pipe-smoking men
in coffee houses and taverns

Practitioners in physiognomy
—the art of studying faces

To prove their skill
they might approach their subject
and say:
"Forgive my intrusion, but
by your brow, you must be a scholar.
Would I be correct, Sir,
in my ascertainment?"

Eyes no longer hold as they used to
Maybe back then the smoke,
or lack of corrective lenses,
softened directness

Or perhaps consciousness was
not yet over-developed,
less likely to quiver when touched

Living in HD fragility
even our eyes
can break egg shells

The Black Magus moved his finger up and down the lines. The writing showed a new range: the attention-getting declaration at the top, an erudite historical allusion, the deft maneuvering to a finely-honed insight. His finger moved back to a particular line. *Eyes no longer hold as they used to.* This was potentially something big and he made a note of it.

But his finger stayed longest on another line: *There were once pipe-smoking men.* The innocuous line saddened him and he wasn't sure why. He blocked the first part of the sentence so that he could only read *pipe-smoking men*. It made him just as sad. No one in his family ever smoked a pipe, so his sadness couldn't be personal. On his notepad he jotted: *Why do I miss pipe smoking men?*

Jerome read the Black Magus' writing.

Up or Forward?

Medieval man
Only looked upward,
To heaven and God

When movement is perceived as only vertical
It is best to stand in one place
So God always knows
Exactly where you are

We
Look and move
Only forward
One direction across flatness

When life is strictly horizontal
The sky is unimportant
The deep earth too

Better than heaven:
To be a fast-moving surface speck

Jerome sounded one line in his head: *It is best to stand in one place.* He looked around the sparse rooms. *If there is a God, God knows exactly where to find him.*

They rotated the writings without comment to the person on their left. When finished reading and making notes, they repeated a third time. They discussed the writings tepidly, with long pauses in between. Natalija's only comment to Jerome was that she loved his reference to Matisse. The Black Magus told Natalija how much he liked the line "Eyes can't hold as they used to," and that he was adding it to a list of "numinous phrases" he wished to explore further. He was about to comment on the puzzling sadness of "pipe-smoking men" but felt an emotional twinge and refrained. He turned to Jerome, held out a hand and patted the air as if feeling for Jerome's personal space.

"Are you blessing me?" Jerome asked.

"I am sensing a temperature change in you. A warming."

Jerome, intrigued, waited for more; but the Black Magus retracted his hand and jotted notes. Natalija wanted to ask The Black Magus about his reference to God but every time she opened her mouth she suddenly felt tired, as if the air inside the triangle was humid and thick. Peripherally she noticed an ongoing nervous habit of Jerome's: he reflexively patted his pockets for his cell phone even though he always left it in his car.

After a few minutes of making notes and loud nasal breathing, the Black Magus addressed his pupils. "Would you like to join me in glimpsing Death's small intestine?"

Jerome pursed his lips. "It's not something I would think to add to my bucket list."

Natalija artistically extended an unfurling hand. "Can you....tell us a bit more?"

The Black Magus brought his fingertips together. "In adolescence I used to have nightmares of tornadoes, black funnels chasing me down. They have returned. What has re-activated them? This time they are smaller, tamer. I allow them to get close, as if inviting a wild animal to feed from my hand. My goal is to entice one close enough to peek up its funnel, into Death's large intestine."

"A guided visualization?" Natalija asked.

The Black Magus clutched his head. "Visualizing is all I've ever done!" He brought his hands down. "It's time to swap the meta-physical for the physical. My dreams are telling me I must get up from my chair and extend my hand." Natalija and Jerome straightened. The Black Magus was veering from his carefully choreographed weekly structure. He pointed at a front window: "I used to live a mile from Lake Erie. Every few years I was lucky to glimpse a waterspout. October is a good time for spouts, when cold air scuds across the still warm lake. When nipples form under the dark bottomed clouds, spouts descend to suckle the lake's summer energy."

The Black Magus stared thoughtfully, then brought his fingertips back together. "The lake is three miles away. I will watch the sky above it. When I see udders form under the lake clouds, Tony will alert you. We will meet at Headlands Beach, lock arms, and peer into Death's large intestine."

"A field trip?" Natalija said, raising and dropping her shoulders. "Cool."

"Do we need permission slips?" Jerome asked, extending the analogy. He felt it was okay to be sarcastic. What were the chances of the Black Magus anticipating a waterspout, alerting them, and all of them converging in time to see it? Zero.

Chapter 9

The Book of Insecurities

Visiting President Garfield

It was a warm, pleasant mid-October afternoon and Natalija decided to take her notebook over to the Garfield Memorial Monument to compose her writing for that week.

Stately oaks and maples sifted a light breeze, animating each red or gold leaf. She sat on the broad limestone steps leading to the entrance of James A. Garfield's medieval-looking presidential tomb. The green park-like lawn, interspersed with shady trees and shrubbery, sloped graciously away from her toward Euclid Avenue far below. Grey mausoleums glinted between the trees like small roman temples and, to her far right, a giant obelisk piercing the trees marked the grave of another famous Clevelander, John D. Rockefeller, Sr.

The last time she was there had been on her 30th birthday two months earlier. She didn't know anyone else who would do such a thing: spend their birthday in a cemetery. She now pondered what she had accomplished in 30 years plus two months. What did she want her life to be like? She wrote down two words: Surface Life. It sounded like a title—the sound of a starting pistol—and she started writing.

Getting delightfully good
at this surface thing
amazed how often I
can float along in my canoe-self
bobbing above the water through
the big water park of life
never splashing anyone
never bumping too hard
not even hearing if water drips from my paddle
Just floating along
one bobbing person
in a flotilla of bobbers

Reading it, she knew such a life was still an enviable fantasy. Had she employed a more accurate metaphor, one of the canoes would have been overturned with her trapped underneath. Clinging to a cross strut inside the darkened canoe and treading water to keep her dripping head above water, she imagined the laughter of the surface people reverberating against the canoe's metal sides. "No canoeist, that one!" Although a few paddlers might sympathetically comment, no one would stop to assist, perhaps assuming specialists were on the way. But at least one thing consoled her. Two things. Her head remained above water. And she was—technically at least—still part of the flotilla.

Typical for a weekday, she had the steps to herself, no other visitors climbing past her to get to the entrance. Poor Garfield. The castle-like tower, blackened from a century and a half of Cleveland steel mills, jutted stoutly at the brow of the hill. According to a docent, most visitors to the tomb came for the views of downtown Cleveland. Maybe that is why she liked Garfield: his canoe, in the flotilla of bobbing presidents, got overturned.

At Garfield's expense, it provided her a silver lining: the steps were all hers. At least the fifth one up on the left. She had thought this might be a good place to compose her writing for *The Book of Insecurity.* But after several scribbled-out starts she wasn't so sure. Then, like a skilled phlebotomist, she teased up a vein.

Twenty minutes later she stood and, not seeing anyone, pivoted to the towering tomb behind her. "Mr. President and Mrs. Garfield." Turning back, she nodded to her right. "Mr. and Mrs. Rockefeller." She then smiled at the downward sloping lawn and the hundreds of grave monuments peeking between the greenery. "Ladies and Gentlemen. It is an honor to bring you a new writing." She cleared her throat, lifted an arm, and began to read in a declamatory voice.

"My Latest Find

How exciting:
I have acquired a new fear!
It will add nicely to my Fear Collection
now large enough
for its first exhibition

My oldest fears, from childhood
will be displayed in glass cases
or where the light is best
Annotation will be provided:
The year a particular fear was acquired
and how it uniquely restricted my life

But my newest acquisition should
be the most featured piece,
spot-lighted on a pedestal
or on wires from the ceiling
a bold statement
that I am open to contemporary works

She raised an arm to acknowledge the cheering monuments below. "Thank yooou, Cleveland. You've been lovely!"

Reaching into Purgatory

Jerome sat in front of his lap top staring at the screen. He was sure his habit of composing on a computer and *then* transposing it by hand would be condemned by the Black Magus. But so far his "pre-machining" had gone undetected. Even so, every week his pleasure in hand-writing the final version increased, leading him to purchase an expensive fountain pen. The scratch of the nib and palpable flow of blue ink made it seem like he was etching himself onto a surface.

But right now nothing was flowing. Frustrated, he randomly typed.

And so
I write poems
spraying words on surfaces
already several inches thick
with hardened paint
from a million spray cans before mine

He envied Shakespeare for having leveraged the largest blank surface ever discovered. Same with the Beatles in music. Where could one possibly find a surface un-caked with writing?

He thought of the Triangulum. Was that a kind of clean surface? What he brought to this week's session would go onto "a canvas", *The Book of Insecurity.* But what exactly did that mean? Despite what Phil Lundy said, would any of the project's writings actually get published? Or was The Triangulum really just a ten-year treadmill powered by two new victims each year to keep a once renowned poet on life support?

And what if the Black Magus' house burned down? Had anyone made copies of the project's accumulated writings?

After a fruitless hour, Jerome resorted to a manilla folder labelled "Purgatory", poems—many composed years ago—which had never made his A-List. He leafed through the folder, scowling from poem to poem until pulling one to read more closely.

Introvert

Every day a hundred tiny concussions
Hardly measurable
But cumulative

Escorting myself off
the 14th floor playing field
I can't remember which decade it is
or correctly count three fingers

At home, I submit
to concussion protocol
It is pointless, confiscating my helmet to
keep me out of the game
—I've already forgotten where I put it!

When asked what I had for lunch

I am so confounded
the question is withdrawn

Sleep can be dangerous so
soon after head trauma
I must instinctively know this
since I never rest deeply

The next morning
I remember where I put my helmet

I am cleared to play

He had never regarded it as more than a drawn-out ditty. Now a new thought occurred: *Natalija might like this*. If she really liked it, she might reach over and touch him. He re-read it trying to remember the writing's context. When he came to the line, *When asked what I had for lunch*, his head went back. It was a favorite question of Sherri's: "So, what did you do for lunch today?" He knew she wanted to know *with whom* he had lunch. When, during the final year of their marriage, his daily answer narrowed to "I had lunch by myself", she finally lost interest.

He released the poem from Purgatory, aligned it next to a clean sheet for transposing, and uncapped the fountain pen, already excited about scribing the nib across the paper's unmarred surface.

Collapsing Sky

An hour before his pupils were to arrive, the Black Magus reviewed the writing which he had previously contributed to *The Book of Insecurities*. Unlike his contributions to the other

Books, this one remained unmodified through the annual re-configurations of the Triangulum. Its soft sediment had long since washed away to hard rock.

Dread

Something hits my roof
A soft thud
And then another

Outside
Black amorphous creatures
Splatter on my patio in a thick torrent
A three-pronged terror
of invertebrates,
a collapsing sky,
and not knowing
if it will stop

He had written it after a downpour so heavy it sounded like living things were splatting on his patio slab. At one point he actually wondered if a waterspout had moved inland, spilling fat carp. When the bombardment increased, he panicked. With nowhere to go, he fled to a childhood fort: he threw a heavy blanket over the dining room table, crawled underneath, and clamped his hands against his ears.

Months later the incident came up in a "maintenance" appointment with Dr. Bakos. To break the routine of their decades-long relationship they had started a game: one or the other would throw a curve ball. At that meeting Dr. Bakos, loading a stapler, casually asked: "You've never told me: what is your greatest fear?"

The Black Magus caught it and pitched it back. "Invertebrates raining from the sky".

Dr. Bakos banged down on the stapler to test it. "I have to say....I've never heard anyone say that."

The Black Magus beamed. "Of course, doctor. Of course."

Chapter 10

The Book of Leaps

Eighth Meeting of the Tenth Triangulum

Red and gold leaves matted the puddles in the Black Magus' driveway. Jerome arrived five minutes before 10, parked, and waited. He liked to be there when Natalija arrived. He liked standing with her under the changing trees. He liked entering the house with her.

Under a blue sky, the tiny orange leaves on the maple seedlings growing in the front gutter looked like a festive banner. He remembered Natalija wondering if they should help. As he waited, he conjured a Saturday morning: the two of them on ladders, pulling tree seedlings from the Black Magus' gutters.

A minute later Natalija's Corolla splashed down the drive, leaves mottling her tires. Jerome got out, acting as if he had just arrived. He wondered which personality-type her hair would forecast for today.

At last week's meeting, their seventh, they had brought their contributions to the Book of Insecurities. Jerome could not remember much about the discussion. Natalija had taken bands of her reddish-blond hair which normally framed her face and looped them to the back of head where they were clipped together. Although simple enough, it made her entrancing. Was this the High-Renaissance look the Black Magus had sometimes referenced? Later he performed an internet search for Botticelli's *La Primavera*. The Black Magus had compared her to the blossom-strewing Flora striding forth on the right. But he felt she better resembled the summer muse furthest left whose head tilted obliquely toward her two sisters as their arms interlaced in an elegant June dance. Despite her entwinement with others, the far-left muse gazed distantly, inscrutably. Like Natalija.

Natalija got out and weakly smiled. Her hair was limp; instead of tossing it with a flip of her head she lifted it back. Notebook crooked against her chest, she sullenly approached.

"I didn't have time for coffee," she said, looking tired. "I wish I could drink his instant."

Jerome, both disappointed and relieved she looked less attractive, smiled. "You might have to. Our topic involves leaping." She made a pouty face and for a second he thought she might rest her forehead against his shoulder. He froze, not wanting to move.

Inside they took their assigned seats and waited for the teacher to enter from the kitchen where a spoon clinked inside a ceramic mug. Jerome leaned toward Natalija. "Last chance for instant coffee." Natalija shivered. The Black Magus ambled into the room, coffee sloshing, but never spilling. After sitting he lifted the steaming cup to his lips, his hand perceptibly shaking.

"Are you okay?" Natalija asked.

"I am quivering with excitement....to find out what has been brought to The Book of Leaps." Natalija sensed deflection. It occurred to her that, despite his being overweight and using a cane, he never complained of physical ailments. *If you took away his legs, he would only see it as an inconvenience. Like a holy man.*

The Black Magus, stabilizing the cup with both hands, turned to Jerome. "What is it you bring to *The Book of Leaps*?"

"That's a good question." Jerome handed out copies of his writing.

Peripheral Vision

Something waves at me from the side
or whispers "Over here"
then vanishes as quickly as I turn

Was there really nothing there?
Or did I just miss it?

Look at the night sky, where the comet should be
Turn your head slowly
until a smudge of light
imprints on the corner of your eye
Turn back, staying with it
and you will see the comet

From now on I will try not to be so jumpy

When something waves at me from the side
or whispers
I will turn more slowly

From the corner of my eye

The Black Magus held an index finger against his chin. "How is turning slowly the same as leaping?"

Jerome dug his fingernails into his palm. This week's assignment had targeted his Achilles heel: he was a trudger, not a leaper. Was the Black Magus calling him out? He opened his mouth, then turned to Natalija, appealing for a second opinion.

Natalija ran a finger over each line, then unbent her head. "To see something you couldn't see before....requires a leap. In movies when someone leaps, it's always in slow motion."

The Black Magus spread fingertips over Jerome's writing as if to confirm, braille-like, Natalija interpretation. He abruptly looked up, his brown eyes boring into Jerome. "When something imprints on the corner of your eye, row for it!"

"Row for it?"

"It could be land."

"Land?"

"You are still too romanced by sinking."

"Sorry?"

The Black Magus resumed sorting papers in his lap. "I want to see calluses on your hands. From rowing."

Jerome glanced at Natalija, hoping to exchange raised brows. She studied the Black Magus with concern. The Black Magus finished jotting notes then tilted his pen at her. "And what do you bring to *The Book of Leaps*?"

"Are we finished discussing Jerome's..."

"Go ahead," Jerome said, trying to look chastened. "While I find some paddles."

"Oars," the Black Magus corrected.

Natalija handed out her handwritten copies and they bowed their heads to read.

Mesopotamia

There is a great wind
blowing above the treetops
There is a great river
flowing beneath the roots

It is very confusing
living between two great flowings!

Some days I want to climb the highest tree
until my hair tousles and eyes water
from the roar above

Other days I want to find a low spot
press my ear to the ground
and smile to hear
a very deep humming

But I am getting too old to climb
or lie in ditches

As consolation, I will place
my ear against a large tree–
A syphoner of flowings
from above
and below

Jerome, knowing his fellow pupil's metaphysical pirouettes would appeal to the Black Magus, studied his reaction. The Black Magus removed his glasses and rubbed his eyes.

"You have found it!"

"Found what?" Natalija asked.

"The Golden River."

Natalija's eyes fluttered. "The golden what?"

"The transpersonal river which encircles us." The Black Magus pushed himself out of the chair and ambled from the triangle. Natalija drew a large question mark paired with an exclamation mark on her note pad and flashed it at Jerome.

The Black Magus opened the door to the adjacent back room, entered and partly closed the door behind him. They angled their heads to track his scrounging sounds. A moment later he returned with a book. Re-seated, he opened the book toward them. "Van Gogh" he said, pronouncing the 'gh' as an 'f', "knew of the golden river. He painted it in Starry Night."

Jerome and Natalija instantly recognized the iconic painting of a swirling starry sky over low mountains and a tiny village. The Black Magus ran a finger along a shimmering band of light cascading right to left above the undulating line of low mountains. He smiled at Natalija. "The roar above the trees you heard. The transpersonal river. The Golden River."

She and Jerome, channeling kindergarten story time, edged closer. The Black Magus traced, then retraced, the golden flow above the mountains. His finger stopped at the tip of a miniscule church steeple rising from the tiny village. "The steeple barely breaks the line of the mountains, just enough to pierce the Golden River, connecting it to the village below." The Black Magus grinned, tapping on the spire. "That's the three of us: a slender triangle penetrating the shimmering transpersonal flow above the village."

Jerome, both amused and intrigued by the Black Magus' transformation into a Jungian Mr. Rogers, pointed at the bottom of the picture. "Where is the river that flows below?"

"It is, as you point out, below." He pointed at a dark flame-like shape dominating the left foreground. "A cypress tree. It is a link between the flowings. Van Gogh gave it power by making it the closest object to us. Like Natalija's tree, it mediates between the rivers, above and below."

Natalija twisted her lips. The painting reminded her of Slovenia and the fateful day of The Drop. *Is that what happened?* Some kind of hole—like a tear in the ozone layer—had appeared over the pub garden, exposing her unknowingly to radiation from the transpersonal flow. How could something that left her damaged be a Golden River? "Didn't Van Gogh paint this at a mental hospital?" she asked.

The Black Magus smiled. "You don't need to climb trees, or lie in ditches. You have found a Listening Tree. You must tell others how to use it. You must tell *us*."

Jerome replayed the Black Magus' earlier words. "*The three of us.... penetrating the shimmering transpersonal flow....*" He wiggled his toes inside his shoes. *The three of us!* "Yes," Jerome said to Natalija. "Let us know. Seriously." Their eyes met. Jerome wanted to say: *I will gladly climb a tree with you. Or lie in a ditch beside you.* Something passed between them which he wasn't sure how to interpret. Only that it didn't feel bad. A softening, a melting. *An Opening?*

The Black Magus cleared his throat then handed out his writing. "I am replacing my previous contribution to this book."

"A brand new writing!" Natalija crowed.

The Black Magus handed out his writing and they bowed their heads to read.

Living, Living, Be!

What is this place?
How did you get here?
Did your mother know this would happen?

If you are not more awake than this time last year
Act at once!

Run out the back door, right this minute!
(Even in your underwear!!!)

Rip a pear from your neighbor's tree

Let its juice splash down your chin

Litter a trail of ravaged cores back to the door
From which your madness spilled

You can apologize later

Natalija peered into the kitchen. Moving her head she could see through the window over the sink into the neighbor's yard. In the corner, just before the field, was a mature fruit tree. Ripe green fruits weighed down its branches. Adjusting her view, she noticed a plump pear on the kitchen counter, a small leaf clinging to its stem. She sucked in her lower lip. She had misjudged the Black Magus. He would not be okay if he lost his legs. *He wants badly to run again....and knock things over.*

Chapter 11

The Waterspout

Daylight fluctuating around the window shade prompted the Black Magus to winch himself out of bed faster than usual. *To the north, toward the lake*! He rumbled through his house and opened the front door. Above the red and gold sugar maples a continuous herd of slate-bottomed clouds migrated west to east. Although he couldn't see Lake Erie, three miles away, he knew the clouds were "lake clouds".

Every ten minutes for the next hour he tracked the migration. Blue sky increasingly pierced the herd and he wondered if it was thinning. Then around 7:30am the cloud train thickened again. He stepped out onto his front stoop, his driveway offering a view through the trees to the sky over the lake. Tufts were forming under some of the clouds. The warm lake was trying to tug them down. "Udders*!*" he yelled. He hobbled to the wall phone in the kitchen and called Tony.

"What are you doing today?"

"Meetin' a guy from Detroit at 2 to trade some cards."

"This morning?"

"Nothin'."

"Get here as soon as you can. I'm sniffing a water spout."

The Black Magus dressed, made instant coffee, then rummaged through a closet for shoes suitable for sand. He found a pair of work shoes he remembered wearing his last visit to the lake five years ago. He set out an old army surplus jacket and a dark blue knit cap and then ambled back to a front window. Peering at the sky at the end of his driveway, an udder telescoped downward into a partial funnel before passing behind the trees. The dance partners of sky and water were eyeing each other, sexually charging the atmosphere.

A few minutes later a gold Cadillac splashed down the driveway. The Black Magus intercepted Tony at the bottom of the front steps.

"The ladder is in the back?"

"Ladder?"

"I need you on the roof."

Behind the house Tony positioned a weathered wooden ladder against the gutter. "I'll hold it for you," the Black Magus offered.

"These rungs look pretty dicey."

"It's fine."

"Hey, I'm an old guy too."

Tony crept up the ladder, testing each rung, then carefully climbed onto the roof. His long grey locks blowing west to east, he crawled to the roof ridgeline, indenting his hands and knees into soft patches of moss. Through breaks in the treetops he saw the distant blue line of Lake Erie. Streaming over his head from behind, sunlight spoked fingers into the moving cloud train. One of the beams ignited a distant line of orange leafed maples, flaming them against the slate-blue backdrop. Beyond, bright specks like stars flashed in and out of the beam. *Seagulls?*

"Do you see any udders?" the Black Magus called up.

"Udders?" He slowly stood, steadied himself, and peered over the trees. After a minute, a swirling smoky cloud entered from the left, thickening into a downward pointing white finger. Directly below it, on the lake surface, water churned. A moment later sky and water reached for each other.

"Splash!" Tony yelled. He watched the waterspout track to the right until obscured by trees. A minute later another funnel formed to the left. The lake surface below it boiled and, as before, water and sky reached, connecting halfway into a whirling dervish. Tony scrunched down and crawled backwards to the roof edge. "Hold the ladder!"

Relieved to be on the ground, he rubbed his knees.

"Well?" the Black Magus asked, his pained expression prefiguring disappointment.

Tony placed a hand on his friend's shoulder. "It's a freakin' water spout parade!"

Jerome left his house around 8am and 15 minutes later joined rush hour traffic oozing down Cedar Hill. As the flow slowed, he received a text from an unknown number: *Alert! Waterspouts sighted. On way to Headlands beach.* It took him several seconds to shift his brain from negotiating traffic to understanding the cryptic text.

At the bottom of the hill he worked his car to the right and pulled into a parking lot where he checked his calendar: nothing until a lunchtime meeting with a client. Instead of being excited by the alert he felt heavy. It seemed too difficult to disengage from the tidal pull into the city, drive a half hour in the opposite direction, and *maybe* see a waterspout. Besides, he was wearing a suit. He called the number but there was no pick up. He bit his lower lip and scrolled through his contacts to Natalija. Since she worked the evening shift she might still be in bed at 8:17am. He had never called her and was oddly nervous. Suddenly he saw a solution: If she didn't pick-up, he would text Tony that he couldn't join them. On the fourth ring she cautiously answered.

"Hello?"

"Natalija, hi, its Jerome."

"Oh....hi.

"Did you see Tony's text?" He waited several seconds for a reply.

"No."

"There are water spouts, or *a* water spout, on the lake. Tony and....our teacher....are on their way to Headlands Beach. I'm on my way to work but was thinking of going."

"I'm actually walking down Mayfield. I just dropped my car off for service."

Jerome glanced tensely at his eyes in the rearview mirror. "I can pick you up."

"I'm a few blocks from Coventry," Natalija replied. "East, I think."

"I'll be there in five."

Driving on Route 2 to Headlands Beach, Natalija and Jerome took turns monitoring the clouds scudding to the north, over Lake Erie.

Natalija pointed above a line of yellow and orange canopied trees ignited against the dark backdrop. "I thought I saw a funnel. No.....maybe not."

Flecks of blue perforated the fast-moving cloud deck. "Can you have water spouts when there's open sky?" Jerome asked. Natalija lowered her head to look through his window. Her nearness tingled his whole right side. He realized it had been awhile since anyone else had been in the passenger seat. Her long hair and faded jeans reminded him of driving back to Cornell with his college girlfriend. If they got to the lake, and there were no spouts, maybe they could walk on the beach.

Jerome lifted his phone. "Another text from Tony. 'P-6'. Is that some kind of code?"

"Probably where they're parked"

They pulled into Headlands State Park and turned right down a tree-lined drive. On their left a series of empty, tree-fringed parking lots extended toward a broken line of trees and tall grasses interspersed along low dunes, obscuring the lake.

"We just need to find another car," Jerome observed.

"There!" Natalija pointed. They turned into the P-6 lot and parked next to a gold Cadillac with a Chief Wahoo bumper sticker. They got out and surveyed the low scrubby dunes and thin screen of trees. Jerome looked down the front of himself as if noticing a stain. "What's wrong?" Natalija asked.

"I've never been on a beach in a suit."

Natalija clapped her hands together and laughed. It was the first time he'd heard her really laugh.

"What?" he asked.

She pointed at a nearby sign. "It says no motorized vehicles beyond this point, but nothing about suits." Jerome mockingly primped his tie and they started toward the beach.

At the nearest break in the low dunes, a hydra-headed basswood tree with six writhing trunks guarded a weather-beaten picnic table. A stout figure in a faded green army jacket huddled on a bench, his back to the table, facing the lake. Standing next to him, Tony turned and waved. A broad beach with gray pebbly sand extended for a 100 yards or more to the oceanic lake. Downy seagull feathers skimmed across the sand like blowing snow. A low ridge of sand halfway between them and the lake barely obscured the waves, but they could hear them. For a moment he was unsure where he was, twinging a dormant feeling he struggled to identify.

The Black Magus, frowning under a blue knit hat, looked like a disabled Viet Nam vet. Tony's long grey hair lifted under his Cleveland Indians' hat, his gold ear cuff glinting in the fluctuating sunlight. "I saw two spouts from the house," he said, "going right down the lake west to east, a couple miles out". They gazed silently at the fast-moving, slat- bottomed clouds. A white tuft teasingly swirled under one of them. "You can do it, baby!" Tony yelled. But the tuft soon unraveled.

Natalija sat on the bench and, scooting to the Black Magus, motioned Jerome to sit on her right. Gulls silently wheeled overhead, flashing bright white in sunbeams, the beams extending into the lake and igniting green iridescent bands below its surface. Natalija urged Tony to sit at the other end of the bench next to the Black Magus. She shifted to make room, pressing against Jerome. Tony, estimating a tight fit, knelt next to the bench instead.

Jerome peeked at his bench companions. The Black Magus seemed a different person outside the context of his home, a handicapped person wheeled out to take in the sea air. Natalija wore a Mona Lisa smile, the corners of her eyes and mouth enigmatically upturned. Strands of her red-blonde hair tickled his neck.

"No ships today?" he asked. No one responded. "Do you think the gulls ever cross over to Canada?" When no one answered again, he checked his watch; he would give this fifteen minutes.

Scrubby growth obscured the view to their left. Tony shifted forward to peer around it. "There!" he shouted. They leaned forward as one. A ragged grey cloud with white stripes was dropping from the cloud deck several miles out.

"A funnel cloud!" Natalija shouted.

"Watch the water!" Tony yelled. When the funnel lowered halfway to the surface, the water kicked up. A moment later the funnel thickened to the lake as if an invisible hand had colored it in.

"Oh my God!" Natalija exclaimed. "A tornado!"

"A water spout." Tony corrected.

"Death's large intestine," the Black Magus muttered.

The spout tracked down the lake, a ghostly conduit between cloud and water. It struck Jerome as strangely sexual, a sudden protrusion straining to expend itself. He called over to Tony. "How long will it last?"

Tony pointed. The bottom of the spout thinned then lifted. The funnel lingered for a half minute before breaking into wisps.

Jerome turned to Natalija. "Wow!"

Natalija's eyes darted like a little girl's eyes searching for the next Christmas present. She leaned off the bench to peer around the scrubby vegetation. "Oh my God!" Another funnel cloud careened around the headland, much closer than the first. Within seconds a rope of water angled towards the sky.

"Splash!" Tony cried. "Geezus, that's only a mile out!" The shifting sun spokes, slanting from behind them, weakened, cooling the air around them. "Listen!" Tony exclaimed. Jerome and Natalija cocked their heads.

"Its like wind through trees," Jerome said.

"Like water from a fountain, pattering onto pavement," Natalija added.

The spout skated left to right, then wobbled, gouging up more spray.

"It's seen us!" The Black Magus cried. Its speed increased, vectoring across the wind.

"I think it's getting closer!" Jerome yelled. He turned to Tony, the group's ostensible science officer. "Tony?"

"It does appear to be closing in proximity," Tony matter-of-factly confirmed. Jerome knew that waterspouts broke up after hitting land. But not immediately. His heart started pounding and he stood.

"We should get back from the beach."

Natalija took his hand and drew him back to the bench. She hooked her arm through his, then did the same to the Black Magus on her left, prying an opening above his pocketed right hand. She signaled Tony to do the same. Still kneeling at the other end, Tony placed his right hand on the Black Magus' shoulder. Anchored to each other, they watched the water spout approach.

The blue-white dervish whirled and careened, blasting up water. Because it was alone on the lake it was hard to get a sense of its scale. Only that it was getting bigger.

To suppress panic, Jerome closed his eyes. He sensed his bench companions through his intertwined left arm. They were an immeasurable nothing against this. But somehow *something*. He suddenly felt great affection for them. Tiny words he had read seven weeks ago reappeared: *Make the Leap. Love. Surrender*. His face spasmed and, startled that he was about to cry, he turned away, pretending something was in his eye. To his right, several feet away, a seagull stood on one leg, gazing imperturbably at the spout. It made Jerome want to laugh. He nodded at the gull, then turned back and lifted his face towards Death's large intestine. *Let it come. We are here!*

Suddenly he lost all sense of himself, his weight ripping from the bench and yanked across the water into the spout. But no, he was still here, his arm entwined with Natalija's. He was seamlessly both observer and participant: A Beholder. *I have never known this.*

Tony pointed. "Look!"

As if snagged by a giant hook, the funnel tore from the water. It flailed in their direction, its open bottom flashing green before retracting as a smoking funnel. The water surface beneath it un-wrinkled. As the disintegrating funnel hurtled eastward, Jerome serenely felt his weight again. The gull next to him took flight, flashing in a new sunbeam. Jerome closed his eyes, squeezing out moisture.

They silently waited for what the lake and sky might deliver next. To the west, blue sky increasingly perforated the cloud deck. The Black Magus spoke for the first time.

"When it bent from the water, it pointed at me."

"What are you talkin' about?" Tony asked.

"Death's large intestine....motioned at me."

Tony rubbed his chin. "That's funny—I thought it was pointin' at me!" He turned to Natalija and Jerome, and winked.

Chapter 12

The Book of Reconnecting

The Coffee Shop

Over the next two days Jerome continually re-played events and how everything had aligned: how he was able to pluck Natalija from the sidewalk, how on the bench they all hooked arms, the steadfast sea gull; how, in a moment of panic, he found calm. Found *others.* As soon as he stopped living ahead of himself the waterspout changed directions, no longer a threat. He even felt love for the seagull, wanting to go back to the beach to look for him.

He replayed the car ride back from the beach, how Natalija kept saying "Wow!" The only crimp came when they discussed the Black Magus.

"Why," Jerome said, "did he have to personalize an awesome natural spectacle into a morbid portent? Isn't that narcissistic?"

Natalija looked out her window, then through the windshield. "If he thought an angel pointed at him, *that* would be narcissistic. But he thought it was Death."

Her words reminded him of a structural difference between them. If he intellectualized enough about something, he might get to it, at least closer. She seemed to get there another way, and he wasn't sure how.

On Wednesday, the day before the Triangulum's next meeting, Jerome received a text from Tony saying the meeting was cancelled. The Black Magus wasn't feeling well.

Jerome sat at his desk, stunned. Luke Thompson entered his office and, observing Jerome's face and his listlessly held cell phone, froze.

"Everything okay?"

"Not sure."

"I'll stop back. Not important."

Jerome sat stricken for several minutes then jerked upright. He pulled up Natalija's number and texted: *Do you still want to meet tomorrow anyway? Coffee shop Coventry? 10 am?* Maybe the planets hadn't finished aligning for the week. Not expecting an immediate response, he went to go see what Luke wanted.

Throughout the day Jerome kept an eye on his phone, even peeking during meetings. He thought about calling but—his thumb hovering over Natalija's number—he held back. When he went to bed that night he intentionally left his phone in the kitchen, tired of beseeching it for a sign. After turning out the light and closing his eyes he heard the Black Magus' anguished cry from an earlier meeting: *Just one drop of moisture. One drop!*

The next morning as his Keurig powered up he checked his phone and was surprised to see a text from Natalija. It simply said Okay.

"Okay," he repeated. "Okay!"

At 9:55 he arrived at the coffee shop in Coventry where they had first met, bought a coffee and took it to an uncrowded corner. With a view of the door, he started checking his work emails. At 10:01 he started glancing at the door. Whenever it swung open, he was careful not to immediately look up in case it was her. By 10:07 he was looking up anytime somebody walked past the storefront window. At 10:10 he received a text from Natalija: "Sorry."

"Sorry what?" But he knew. He drained his cup and left.

As he drove down Mayfield he realized he was approaching the spot where, the previous week, he had pulled over to pick up Natalija for the waterspout adventure. He avoided looking and wanly smiled. "You, sir…are one needy bastard." He pressed on the accelerator, bending himself toward work. Away from moisture.

Black Dog

The Black Magus, instant coffee in hand, pondered the overcast sky. The deep depression which led to a rare cancellation of last week's Triangulum session had finally slipped from his shoulders. The black dog still lurked—in a closet or under furniture—but at least he could step around it.

A burst of lake effect snow descended on the field like a horde of locusts. He liked that the flakes were of lake water, the northwest wind scooping moisture from Lake Erie then—colliding with the escarpment east of Cleveland—jarring loose as snow. The lake, which he now held sacred, was coming to him.

When the waterspout flailed, the greenish light which flashed from its up-turned bottom provided a worm-hole view to a distant place. He had never thought of eternity as having a color. Now he knew: it was pale green. Such a thing witnessed in his youth would have supported his mother's belief, expressed to him after she came upon some of his first poems, that he was somehow *chosen*. Now, it led to deflation. Death was approaching. Close enough to be viewed from a picnic table at Headlands Beach.

After a week of struggling to pull himself from the undertow he found something to grab onto: he would add an 11th folder to the ten folders currently aligned across the utility table. But it would be his own. The epiphany instantly improved his spirits. And he had a neighbor to thank for it.

Two days ago Paige Wilson, the only neighbor he still knew, appeared at his front door. "I wanted to ask you a favor," the diminutive 86 year old announced. She declined to come in and he joined her on the stoop. "They tell me I have cancer. I've arranged, when I'm gone, for my five cats to be put to sleep. If one of them is overlooked, will you...." She paused to collect herself. "If one is overlooked, please take it to the vet—the one on 306—to be put down. I don't want any of my cats to die outside my house, wondering why I no longer let them in."

He took her hand in both of his. "I promise."

After she left it troubled him that he possessed nothing as precious as Paige's cats were to her. But then he realized he did: his thought-scraps. Jotted on various size pieces of paper, the best ones—those retaining a numinous glow—continued to incubate in the Reliquary. He imagined his sister Rachel in Arizona sending in a thuggish cleaning crew after his death. The image of his thought-scraps ending up in sealed black trash bags horrified him. Better to instruct Tony to euthanize them in a backyard fire. Or maybe....someone might "take them in". If given their own folder, his orphaned thoughts—at least the still-glowing ones—might survive him.

Satisfied with the turn of events, he thunked his cane on the wood floor, a reminder to the black dog that it needed to depart. Another thought further eased his despair. Two more sessions of the Triangulum remained, two more books to complete. *The gods dare not end my odyssey with the home shores of Attica in sight.*

Pedalling his slippered feet in the air, he decided there was time, before his pupils arrived, to play Beethoven's late stringed quartets. It might be the sharp stick needed to prod the black dog out the front door.

Ninth Meeting of the Triangulum

Natalija pulled into the Black Magus' driveway and braked for a freakish burst of late October snow spilling from a low gray cloud. It didn't surprise her. This was a special place where magical things could happen.

She gazed sadly down the drive. One week from now would be their final session. She imagined herself driving past the house in Winter, no longer sanctioned to pull in. Suppressing dread, she proceeded down the drive and parked. She wondered if she should wait for Jerome to tell him how she had walked to within ten feet of the coffee shop and turned around. She didn't want any acrimony to carry into their second-to last Triangulum session. She studied herself in the rearview mirror. Her hair looked unusually red as it did this time of year, deepening—she liked to think— with the fall colors. Jerome's blue Audi glided alongside. She pretended to sort items before getting out.

Jerome was wearing his handsome blue overcoat. Barely glancing her way, he gave a tight-lipped nod and started for the house, then abruptly halted. He cocked an ear toward the front door. "Is that music?"

Natalija came alongside. "Classical music."

"I'm surprised he has the technology."

Despite the cold weather, the front door was partly open and they entered. On the dining room table a "boom box" blared classical music. The Black Magus sat in his Triangulum chair, eyes closed. Despite the intrusion of cold outside air he still wore a short sleeve blue work shirt.

"Good morning," Natalija said. He remained motionless. They stood blinking in the loud music. She instinctively studied his chest, detecting a slight heave. "We're here!" She went over to his chair and, about to nudge him, turned to Jerome. "I don't know what to call him," she mouthed.

Jerome shrugged. "Mr. Magus?"

She touched the large man's shoulder. "Sir?"

The Black Magus' eyes sprang open. Seeing Natalija, his startled look softened. "How pleasant: to be awakened by the Goddess Flora."

"No blossoms today," Natalija replied, showing empty hands.

"Do you always keep your front door open for the first snow? Jerome asked.

"An escape path, for something unwanted to leave. I think it has. You may close the door."

Jerome wondered if furnace-generated heat—a machined quality—was unwanted.

"Do you recognize the music?" the Black Magus asked, sounding congested.

Jerome shrugged. "A string quartet?"

"One of Beethoven's last. Previously when he composed he leveraged the mammalian part of his brain. These come from the new brain, which involved a crossing over. As in all crossings, sublimity occurs."

Jerome, surprised at the Black Magus' pre-session verbosity, wanted to keep the conversation going. He was familiar with Beethoven's symphonies, enough to know the 7th was his favorite. But he wasn't sure how to respond to composing as either "mammalian" or "new brain". He opted for levity. "You have crossed over too," he said, glancing at the boom box.

To his surprise the Black Magus chortled, almost a giggle, then motioned for him to turn it off.

Natalija wondered why he was acting oddly. Almost happily. *Cold medicine?* She had questions she wanted to ask him. What sort of "bug" did he have that caused him to cancel last week's session? Did he have any follow-up comments on their highly eventful field trip to the lake? But she held off, waiting to see if he would respond unprompted. Jerome seemed to be on the same page and they settled silently into their chairs, leaving space for the teacher. Ignoring their quiet invitation, he opened the folder on his lap then thumped his hands on the chair arms.

"Today we bring writings for *The Book of Reconnecting*. What do you bring?"

Jerome and Natalija looked at each other, unsure whether to comply or prod him with questions about the past two weeks. Jerome could tell from her eyes that there was something else. *Good. She should feel bad.*

"I guess I'll go," Jerome said. He handed out his writing and they bowed their heads to read.

A Different Breeze

Sunlight sparkling through May trees
a different breeze touches my face
Something in the past has been disturbed
and picked up in the wind

Like dandelion seeds breaking away
the bits of past float and sail
tickling around my eyes
stirring deep deposits
grains of sand
from my own primordial beach

Natalija reached over and touched his forearm. "That was really good!" she enunciated silently. *Nice of you to say*, he thought. *But why did you stand me up last week?*

The Black Magus removed his glasses then replaced them. "Why don't we read all the writings before we discuss." Natalija handed out her sheet.

The Burying

Ash continues floating down
from some nearby Vesuvius

Favorite paths compress into pyroclastic layers
until I am walking several inches higher
than this time last year

A friend reminds me of something long forgotten
Has that much ash really fallen?

When I retire
don't ask me about My List
I want to become an archaeologist
and excavate my life room by room
like Pompeii

Hitting something hard
I drop my shovel,
get on all fours,
lower my head
and blow

As ash scatters
A corner of a mosaic is revealed:
a floor, where I once stood

Jerome was reminded again of their differences: he, a plodding workhorse, one furrow at a time; and she with a lighter wand, leaving sparkles in her wake. *Like Flora trailing blossoms.* He turned and caught her eye. “Really good,” he lip-synced.

The Black Magus held their writings side by side. “Both of you reference things floating. One is particulate that covers the past. The other *is* the past.” He pressed an index finger to his chin. “In Van Gogh’s Wheat Field, crows hover above the field, intermediaries between the earth and sky.” They waited for him to expand on the cryptic remark. Instead he passed out his writing.

Reconnecting

When I used to go fishing with Tony
I feared catching a fish, knowing
I would have to grip its
Scaly tense aliveness
In order to remove the hook

But I always went when invited

It did me good to hold in my bare hand
The silent primal screaming
That still swims
In the oldest part of my brain

Jerome saw a chance to remedy his missed opportunity to capitalize on the Black Magus’ pre-session loquaciousness. “You said Beethoven’s later quartets came from the new brain. But in your writing you value connection to the old brain.”

The Black Magus grinned. “Neurosis occurs when we lose touch with our original slithery-ness.” He pointed to his right.

"There is a fat toad who lives in my garage. If I had the discipline to cup him in my bare hands every morning, I wouldn't need pills."

Jerome jotted on his pad: *Toad therapy*?

The Black Magus arranged all three writings on his lap. Perusing Jerome's, he penciled a box around the last three lines.

"Why did you do that?" Jerome asked.

"They struck me."

"In a good way? Or bad?"

The Black Magus sniffled. "They are worth returning to." He lay a hand down on the writings, spreading his fingers. "Reconnecting involves a *crossing-back*. It can be accomplished by detecting a certain type of breeze, by digging at a place where one once stood, or by gripping a cold-blooded creature." He suddenly frowned and turned to Natalija. "Your mosaic. What is below it?"

"I don't know."

"Then why not keep digging?"

"That would destroy the mosaic."

A lively conversation ensued between Natalija and the Black Magus, the student defending the preservation of "her mosaic" against the teacher's concern that it blocked a deeper crossing. As the two tussled, Jerome re-examined the three lines of his writing which the Black Magus had highlighted. *Yes, they indicate a crossing-back. He likes crossings. Sublimities. Did I write something sublime?*

The Black Magus ended discussion at 10:55. "Next week.... our final meeting: the tenth meeting of the Tenth Triangulum. There will be no topic. Instead, there will be a place." He reached for a Styrofoam cup and extended it to Natalija. "Pick one." She withdrew a small folded piece of paper and he offered the cup to Jerome who did the same. "What numbers do you have?" They unfolded their scraps.

"Two," Natalija said.

"One," said Jerome.

The Black Magus nodded. "Then I must be three." Jerome, having taken the only piece of paper left in the cup, realized only two had been put in. The Black Magus, in an unprecedented move, handed them each another writing. "Please read."

The Clearing

When you enter The Clearing
Stop running
Against all instinct
Turn to see
What is chasing you

Resist the urge to pick up a sharp stick
Or climb a tree
Spread your arms and open your hands
Let the blood hounds come

Here they are, at the grassy edge–
No longer barking, tongues hanging
This is the moment to bring them water
Do not try and pet them
They do not wish to be walked on your leash!

While the hounds slake
Turn
and walk
They will not follow

They are bred only to chase
Those who are running away

"This writing," the Black Magus said, "introduces you to The Clearing. It is an important place. That is all I can tell you. For next week, based on the numbers we drew, Jerome will write about what happens there next. Natalija, you will write about what happens after what Jerome writes about. I will go last."

Jerome and Natalija frowned, waiting for comprehension. "So," Jerome said, holding his pen out, "How can she follow up on what I write about if she doesn't read mine first?"

"You are in a space where you have stopped running. Two others, one at a time, will come to that space after you. That is all I can tell you."

"Are the hounds still there?" Jerome asked.

"Maybe they went home," the Black Magus answered. "Or maybe their bones are there. That is for you to decide."

Natalija fidgeted. "How big is this place?"

The Black Magus's nostrils enlarged. "I can tell you only this—there is a machete in The Clearing. Maybe it is stabbed into the ground. Or maybe you are holding it! That is up to you to decide."

Outside, Jerome and Natalija walked silently from the house, a coating of slushy snow slopping underfoot. They paused near their cars. "Why would a machete be needed in a clearing?" Natalija asked.

Jerome surveyed some nearby shrubs. "This place needs a machete."

Wind rattled brittle leaves in a nearby oak. Red leaves floated down from a maple, intermixing with lingering snowflakes. Natalija smiled at him weakly, her eyes trying to say something.

"What happened last week?" Jerome asked. "Why didn't you show?"

Natalija looked down, then up at him with a pained look. She turned and pulled a leaf from the top of her car and rolled the stem between her fingers. She stepped over to the car hood, thinly coated with melting snow. Pressing an index finger into the slushy film, she drew an equilateral triangle. Jerome gazed at it. He wanted to see what her eyes were saying but instead slowly nodded at the triangle.

"Well....See you in the clearing. Or, technically, not." He abruptly turned and, before getting into his car, glanced at the lawn, deep green grass blades piercing the snow glaze and levitating a scattering of fallen red leaves, three seasons converging in this strange place. Everything but blossoms.

Chapter 13

The Clearing

When Jerome splashed down the Black Magus' driveway the following Thursday, he smiled at the rhythmic bottoming of his shocks, surprised he had grown affectionate toward the un-machined driveway and its omnipresent puddles.

It was a nice day for the first week in November, warm enough to smell squashed green apples from an unseen tree. Sunlight sparkled through bare branches. He gazed at the house and its familiar aura of flecked paint around the foundation. "The last meeting of the Triangulum Project," he announced aloud, seeing his breath. "What will happen today?" He squinted at the trees. "What will happen after?"

A moment later Natalija arrived. Instead of her usual blue jeans and long sweater she wore a long blue coat which, unbuttoned, revealed a patterned dress, nylons, and nice shoes. One knee turned slightly inward as she walked.

"You look nice," he said. She had even put on a little rouge and eye shadow which—because of its inexpert application—Jerome found endearing. He fought back an urge to step closer.

"Thank you," she replied, tossing back her unbound hair. She perused Jerome, pointing at his tie. "So do you. A client meeting?"

"You got it."

Natalija gazed at the house, her deep green eyes saddening in the clear autumn light. Jerome felt it as a stomach punch: *I will never see her eyes like this again.*

They walked silently across the worn gravel, their steps awkwardly in unison. Jerome lifted his hand to knock and, realizing it would be the last time, stopped. Natalija grabbed his forearm and pushed his closed hand against the door twice. For a moment their eyes met. They entered the house for the last meeting of the Triangulum Project.

The Black Magus sorted a folder in his armchair. With the outside light less obscured by foliage, the room seemed brighter. Natalija and Jerome hovered between their chairs as they had on the first day. When the Black Magus looked up he did a double take, his eyes darting between them.

"You look good together," he blurted.

Natalija blushed.

"It's a special occasion," Jerome quipped.

The Black Magus motioned them to sit. "Please." The gesture, after nine meetings, seemed oddly formal. They draped their coats over the chair backs and sat. Natalija crossed her legs but, reminded of her dress, uncrossed them, tugging the hem over her knees.

The Black Magus interlocked his fingers and squeezed his hands together. His eyes fluttered. "This…is an important occasion: the last time we will meet within The Triangulum." Jerome tilted his head. *Within the Triangulum? Will we be meeting with-out* it?"

The Black Magus, hands still together, turned to Jerome. "You were the first to enter The Clearing. What happened?"

Jerome passed out copies of his writing and they bowed their heads to read.

The Clearing

To my right
the front edge of the Present
a jungle wall

On my left
its back edge,
a vaporous undertow
smelling of damp stone

I am between the two
In the middle of The Clearing

Most of us live on its leading edge
When a young person is handed a machete
it makes no sense not
to face into the glimmering undergrowth
of the next moment

The ground is sandy
But I cannot sit

Is this a place to pace within?
Or pray within?

In its dead calm
there is no place to hide

The Black Magus jotted notes without—to Jerome's disappointment—underlining or boxing any of his lines. The Black Magus nodded to Natalija. "Let us read all before we discuss." Natalija distributed her writing.

The Clearing

Daylight fluctuates
as if through high windows

I haven't sat cross-legged this many hours
since kindergarten

I scratch myself a lot
My back aches

Am I waiting too strenuously?

I can't help eyeing the machete next to me
Was it a mistake to stop moving forward?

My heart starts to race
I swat at my arm
but there is no mosquito

I can't stop glancing at the machete!

Maybe it's best
to start flailing again

Jerome underscored a line, *I swat at my arm, but there is no mosquito.* It bothered him that visceral references eluded him.

The Black Magus shifted uncomfortably. He picked up Jerome's writing and read it side by side with Natalija's. Natalija craned forward. "Did we not follow your instructions?"

The Black Magus looked at the ceiling, as if allowing his eyes to refocus. "Nothing is wrong." He handed out his writing.

The Clearing

Chin slumped to my chest
I hear it before my eyes open:
A low moan which crescendos into
a high pitch wailing

It makes me want to get up and run

But the disturbing sound turns, then
beautifully curves

It has become music!

My head jerks back as if struck by perfume
At once I know why I have never heard
this instrument before:
It is an old man singing!

The transcendence of unexpected beauty
washes over me

I stand up, almost tripping over
my machete

There is no need to pick it up

The humidity is lifting
The jungle wall parting

After a few minutes the Black Magus removed his glasses, glanced back and forth at his pupil's faces, and smiled. "Well done! We were all there. The exact same place! I believe that's the best one yet." The Black Magus, realizing he had inadvertently implicated prior triangula, stopped smiling and cleared his throat. "Yes, yes, ...we cued off each other like jazz musicians."

Natalija frowned. "But nothing really happened to me or Jerome in The Clearing."

"But you were there. And understood the machete, what it could be used for, and resisted. By the time it was my turn the machete no longer mattered. Your discipline helped set that up." Natalija contorted her face. The Black Magus resumed. "What matters is this: we created a space only *we* know about—an eddy in the flow—and we each spent time there. Having been there, we can go back!"

"But we can never be there at the same time," Natalija replied.

"It's a timeshare" Jerome quipped.

The Black Magus smiled at Natalija. "When I am there, I will know you have been there. By the flower petals strewn on the ground."

"How will you know if I've been there?" Jerome asked.

The Black Magus closed his eyes. "I will see footprints from where you paced. And knee indentations from where you prayed."

"Prayed?" Jerome exclaimed. He wanted to correct him: the reference in his writing to praying was rhetorical. But footprints and knee indentations seemed evidentially equivalent to Natalija's flower petals. Maybe even more substantive. Instead, he opened his hand and placed his fingertips, braille-like, upon the Black Magus' writing. "I don't know what it means—that an old man is singing. But when I return to The Clearing, I will listen for him. I want to hear something 'beautifully curve'".

The Black Magus opened his hands. "Maybe you will hear something even rarer! The important thing is *we all know this place*! It has high windows, it can make one sleepy, the leading edge is jungle wall, we like to sit in the sandy middle, the machete tempts us. Unexpected things can happen....when we stop running." The Black Magus gazed steadily at his two pupils. "You have done well. I am proud."

The compliment bypassed Jerome's brain and draped warmly over his shoulders. Natalija graciously extended an upturned hand. "*You* have done well. Thank you."

The Black Magus beamed, alternately patting his thighs. Jerome and Natalija reddened at the silly look.

"So," Jerome said. "We have established a metaphysical space to return to. But what happens next?" He was deliberately vague. Next could mean any length of time.

The Black Magus pointed a thumb at the back room. "It is time for me to complete the Triangulum Project. Those from the First Triangulum have been waiting ten years."

Natalija had always wanted to ask him about the writers who had come before them, what they were like. She refrained, but not because he had admonished them never to ask. Part of her wanted to think there never had been any others.

Jerome remembered Phil Lundy's comment about the Black Magus not releasing the fellowship manuscripts unless a Brink's truck backed down his driveway. "I'm sure the Literary League can help prepare the manuscripts for publication."

The Black Magus narrowed his eyes. "I have a few things I still need to address."

"Can we help?" Natalija asked.

The Black Magus stared at the floor in the middle, his body perceptibly rocking. "Yes."

Natalija craned forward. "Yes?"

"I do have something to ask, that I have never asked of any other Triangulum." He slowly brought his fingertips together. "We three have constellated well. We have brought back many quiet secrets." He paused and sipped coffee, his hand slightly trembling. "Would you....be willing to come back one more week?" Jerome and Natalija straightened. "Each week," the Black Magus continued, "the terms have been dictated by the Books. What if next week we each bring a writing that does not fit into any Book?" His eyes flashed a sudden sadness Jerome had never seen. Was the Black Magus having Triangulum termination issues?

"I'm good with that," Natalija said, turning to Jerome.

To buy time, Jerome reflexively patted his pockets. "I'll check my schedule. It will probably work."

The Black Magus' eyes moistened and, hands gripping the chair arms, he started to gently rock forward and back.

"Wait! Natalija exclaimed. "There is a condition." She smoothed her dress over her knees and primly rested her hands upon her lap. "I will only come back if you bring a brand new writing."

"With a birth edge," Jerome chimed.

The Black Magus sloughed into a stare, then straightened. "I will sharpen my best pencil."

Natalija crouched forward out of her chair toward the Black Magus and held up her right hand.

"I believe she wants to high-five you," Jerome interpreted. He mimed the motion.

The Black Magus shifted forward, raised his right hand, and Natalija cleanly smacked it.

"Nicely done!" Jerome called out. To his amazement, he started clapping.

Chapter 14

Re-enchantment

The Black Magus awakened to a strange stillness. He could tell from the velvety radiance seeping around the window shade that a clear bejeweled sky was slowly giving way to an indigo eastern light. The milky light slinked into the room and rested atop him like an extra blanket. He twisted to look at the door. It was three quarters closed as he had left it before getting into bed. d.a. had not visited him during the night. But someone else had.

He groaned upright, heaved his legs over the edge of the bed and reached for the pad and his reading glasses. Even in the faint light he could read the nocturnally scrawled words. *Your slender, gentle, motioning arm.* He recognized his code words for the goddess. *She* had been the one to visit him last night.

He had dreamt he was walking through the darkened living room of his childhood home when two hands, one under each armpit, lifted him from behind. He reached back and felt the hands: small and feminine, though hard and rough as if belonging to a weathered medieval statue. He reached up and felt the head behind his: a warm skull with sickly strands of long hair. She carried him upward. On the verge of passing through the wide threshold into the dining room his head bumped against the upper jamb, jolting him from the dream.

In his youth, the goddess had been a beautiful fairy princess. For some reason her horrifically altered appearance didn't alarm him. The skull with patchy hair suggested the moldering body of a female saint, like those encased in glass caskets in Italian churches. He gazed at a picture of a smiling, dark-haired woman on the dresser. "Who was it mother? Saint Agnes? Saint Claudia? Whomever.....I am sure you have had them over for a cup of Lyon's."

But where was the female spirit taking him? Had his heart stopped when her stone hands first clutched him, and then re-started when he bumped his head? Is that why d.a. had not opened his bedroom door, sniffing death more than life? His breathing accelerated. "I have been given a respite. But for how long, and for what? A specific task? Am I meant to brush my teeth, and then die? Or something else? What?!"

He wondered if it had something to do with his students. The Tenth Triangulum had been the most productive and to his surprise his pupils had agreed to return an extra week. Today.

"Damn it," he muttered, remembering his pledge to Natalija of a new writing. Maybe he could substitute one from his Orion Trilogy. He thought of Natalija in her patterned dress from the week before, as if she had stepped from Botticelli's Primavera. "No," he smiled. "You must not deceive a goddess. Even a lesser one."

Still sitting on the edge of his bed he realized he was thirsty. The area around his eyes pleasurably twitched. "Lemonade," he said. *That first Lemonade*! Sensuousness cascaded down his neck into his right arm. When it reached his fingers they convulsed, closing then re-opening as if from an electric current. His eyes narrowed. "Can a hand have ancient memories?" A strange happiness—a commingling of something giddily new with something acutely nostalgic—suffused him.

He felt for his cane, groaned upright, ambled to the window and let up the shade. "This, I have never seen!" Under a brightening eastern sky, ground mist blanketed the field in an other-worldly glow. The mist appeared as a solid layer, as if three feet of snow had fallen during the night. Closer to the house, footprints in the dewy grass approached the window where they paused, turned toward the house, and then resumed, disappearing into the mist. The footprints were large and rounded. He remembered d.a.'s large feet and high-top sneakers. "So, womb brother, you would not even enter my house, much less my room. Have I already started not being here? Already begun to smell?"

He gazed sadly out the window. For a minute he stopped thinking, allowing the dual lusters of ground mist and brightening sky to coat his face and bare arms. Remembering his promise to Natalija, his melancholy eased. If he was to be at his window chair in time to see the sun rising over this strange mist he needed to get dressed, make coffee, and sharpen a pencil. He held out his right hand which was still trying to grip something invisible. The time had come to reach into the Deep Translucent Pond. On this special day he would have the help of two others. Together they might have an arm long enough.

As Jerome drove to the Black Magus' house he recited the only poetic verse he knew by heart:

> "When you see It, don't be too tired
> Move closer until you feel a breeze
> Extend your hand
> If it disappears, you have found an Opening"

He had been near enough to Natalija to detect a breeze from a deep unseen place. But every time he reached for it his hand remained pitifully extended. Maybe it was something intrinsic about himself. An emotional neediness easily spotted? Or was it a question of mechanics: Was he extending his hand incorrectly?

He crackled down the Black Magus' drive, parked, cut the engine and felt the car's hermetic stillness. "After today, I will never see them again." He waited for a reaction, but felt nothing.

Getting out he instantly noted something different. Leaves had been raked or blown from the lawn. The flaked paint ringing the foundation was also gone, probably blown with the leaves. It made the house smaller and duller, as if it had lost its aura. He glanced down the driveway for Natalija's Corolla. Seeing nothing, he walked to the house, dutifully knocked and entered.

The three empty chairs were triangulated as usual. For the first time a folder wasn't neatly positioned on the table beside the Black Magus' chair. "Hello?" After ten sessions he was still unsure what name to call out. *Sir? Teacher? Mr. Magus? Bear?* The door to the back room was open and sunlight angled into the living room. Bending sideways he glimpsed a shoulder clad in a light blue shirt.

"Oh, you're in there." He set his folder on his chair, started to cut through the triangle, stopped, and detoured around it. The Black Magus sat in front of a lone window, his back to Jerome, sunlight slanting across his lap. Jerome rapped the door jamb. "Good morning." The room was barren except for the chair, a small table beside it, book-filled shelves on the left and, against the opposite wall, a six foot long utility table neatly lined with folders. Striations on the wood floor extended laterally from either side of the chair.

Remembering how Natalija had roused the Black Magus from a deep reverie last week, he walked over to the chair. The

Black Magus' eyes were shut and his head slumped forward. His right arm loosely gripping his left arm. Something wasn't right. Jerome studied the man's chest. It didn't move. "Hey! Wake up!" His voice didn't bounce back as it would from a taut, live person. He reached to shake him and, at the last second, shook the chair instead. The Black Magus head slumped further. Jerome jumped back. For some reason he thought of their first meeting at the coffee shop when he had almost stood up and walked away from the Black Magus. Now, twelve weeks later, he was the one to find him dead.

He pulled out his phone and called Tony, his call going into voicemail. "This is Jerome," he quavered. "I'm at his house. You had better come over. Quickly." For good measure he tried a text message, kept making mistakes, and finally just sent it.

Edging back toward the chair he realized he had never seen the Black Magus in sunlight. His face was strikingly unlined, his lashes longer. His hair was greyer than in the dimmer living room. Jerome looked away. Even in death, eyelids closed, eye contact with the other man was daunting. He noticed a yellow pencil on the floor, reflexively picked it up and set it on the table.

The front door opened. "Hello!" It was Natalija.

"In here," Jerome called in a waxy voice.

Natalija set down her folder and entered the room. She observed Jerome's ashen face and the slumped figure in the chair. She quickly walked over and placed two fingers on the side of the Black Magus' neck and watched his chest. Jerome, hands in his coat pockets, stared at the floor. After what seemed a long time, Natalija put her ear to his chest. A half minute later she unbent and stepped back.

"He's gone," she whispered. Her face quivered and she clutched her cheeks. "He believed in me!" She stared out the window, swiping tears with her hands.

Jerome wanted to move closer and comfort her. But he was standing behind the Black Magus on the right while she stood equidistantly behind him on the left. He still felt the triangle.

"I tried to contact, Tony," Jerome said. He took out his phone. "Oh....he just texted. He's on his way." After a silence, he pointed at the Black Magus. "You don't think he….I mean he wouldn't set us up like this."

Natalija blinked away tears. "It looks like a heart attack. His posture." She touched the half full coffee mug on the table. "And why would he make coffee….if he wanted sleep?"

They gazed out the window at a small backyard and, beyond it, an overgrown field, tall brown grasses variously bent. Patches of ground mist dissipated upward. "What do you think he looked at every day?" Jerome asked, frowning at the unremarkable scenery.

Natalija sniffled. "It's all he needed. A window."

Jerome glanced at the lateral marks on the floor, scarred whitely into the brown hardwood planks. "A man gazes out the same window for decades and suddenly it stops. Shouldn't there be ramifications?"

Natalija gazed at the green strong box on the small table beside the chair and read the label aloud. "Reliquary". She slowly lifted the lid. Jerome moved closer. The box was filled with some old photographs and small objects. She pointed at a military medal, a silver star. "His father's."

Jerome pointed at a Rosary. "That surprises me."

"His mother's, I think." She reached, hesitated, then retrieved a black and white photograph. It showed a family of four standing in front of an old house with a front porch. A bald man in a white t-shirt, cigarette jutting from a corner of his mouth, held a rake in one hand, his other arm draped around a young teenage girl in shorts and a blouse. On the porch steps a young boy in shorts and a tucked-in shirt bashfully leaned against a pretty, smiling woman in a simple everyday dress. Natalija pointed at the boy. "Him."

"He's just a shy boy," Jerome said. On the back of the photograph was penciled verse in the Black Magus' hand.

They know they are a family
and live in this house
Leaves are falling and must be raked
A roast is in the oven
They can already smell it through the screen door

Natalija replaced the picture and reverently closed the lid. "Sorry," she said to the Black Magus. "We didn't mean to pry." Pushing away more tears, Natalija turned to the utility table against the wall. On it they counted eleven neatly aligned folders. She walked over and Jerome followed. Each folder had a hand-written label; the furthest to the left was labelled *The First Triangulum*, the next, The *Second Triangulum*, following in order to ten.

Jerome randomly opened the seventh folder. It contained 30 writings which followed the order of the Books. The two pupils of that Triangulum had contributed twenty writings, ten apiece, one for each book. Also included were the Black Magus ten writings, the same, with minor changes, that he had contributed to their sessions. The last two sheets in the folder were skilled drawings in colored pencil. Jerome lifted the first, which showed a middle-aged woman with short dark hair warming her hands on a small, playhouse-size greenhouse containing a potted flower. In the upper right were five elegantly penned lines:

Virtue should never be part of a strategy

Like a delicate orchid
it dwells year round
in a greenhouse
you spent many years constructing

The other drawing featured a close up of a bare-chested man in bed, hovering over his lover, an African-American male. Jerome recognized Hank Tanaka. Instead of looking down into his lover's eyes, he stared to the side. Two lines of verse read:

Even now, I can't help wondering:
What maintenance is scheduled for today?

The next folder also included 30 writings and two drawings. The first drawing surrealistically showed a naked young man clinging desperately to the inside edge of a giant funnel.

And then, The Spiral:
The downward pull into a narrowing spout

The second drawing was a close up of an older woman's face, her eyes soporifically closing. Large, six-pointed snowflakes festooned the air around her, one crumpling against her cheek.

Snowflakes falling so slowly on a windless morning
I am sedated for an entire week

"*He* drew these?" Jerome said.

"Yes," Natalija answered. They opened other Triangulum folders which also contained 30 handwritten writings and two colored-pencil drawings based on two of the writings. As before, ten of the writings were from the Black Magus', updated drafts of the same writing. Going from folder to folder they could see the changes he made.

"It's strange to see the handwriting of previous participants," Natalija said.

Jerome poked at a drawing. "The drawings are all based on his pupil's writings. None from his."

"Maybe he was waiting for the final versions of his ten contributions."

They opened the folder marked, *The Tenth Triangulum.* The writings, theirs, were divided into the same Book groupings as in the other folders. Natalija flipped the loose sheets. At the back of the folder were two drawings sketched in black pencil, apparently studies for a more complete picture. The first showed a young woman with long flowing hair, her head pressed against a large tree. Finely penned lines to the side read:

A syphoner of flowings
From above
And below

"That's you", Jerome said, pointing at the figure.

"It is!" Natalija smiled. A second sketch showed a view downward through tree branches to a man lying on his back in a sleeping bag. The supine figure stared wide-eyed up into the tree. To one side of the drawing yellow shading indicated early morning light. The accompanying verse read:

First sunlight paints branches orange
The tiny movements of a sparrow amaze me
How have I never seen this?

"You," Natalija said, pointing at the face.

Jerome's lower lip quivered. "I guessed he liked it. I had no idea."

Natalija searched the folder for a drawing based on any of the Black Magus' writings but, as with the other folders, there were none. Next to the Tenth Triangulum folder was a bulging folder secured with two rubber bands. On the front was a handwritten title: *The Deep Translucent Pond.* Jerome removed the bands and opened it. It contained various scraps of paper with jotted verses or prose. He and Natalija randomly lifted and read some of the scraps then carefully replaced them as if fragments of papyrus. The last item in the folder, the only one with a title, was on badly-crinkled paper. Natalija, supporting the limp sheet with both hands, angled it to the window light and read aloud.

"Re-Enchantment

Infuse me
Fill me with your ancient breath
Bleed the spent black fluid
hot from my ears
Let it run thick and rancid
Collapsing my starched white collar

Jab me with a wand
Strike open my eyes
Make me see:
The aura around every living thing
The energy pulsing between stars
The gods racing along a burning cloud edge
Your slender, gentle, motioning arm

Finally, at twilight, beneath old trees:
The Deep Translucent Pond
From the bottom, old swords glimmer
Relics
of an earlier light"

Jerome touched the wrinkled paper. "He must have handled this thousands of times."

"Anything read that many times is profound," Natalija said. "Even if only read by one." She returned it to its place and closed the folder.

"The Deep Translucent Pond," Jerome said. "Why label a folder of miscellaneous scraps after a line that appears in the last stanza of a poem buried at the very back?"

Natalija tugged his sleeve. "Follow me."

They went down the thinly carpeted hallway and entered a darkened bathroom. Natalija found the light switch and two florescent tubes on either side of a vanity mirror blinkered to life. The room had the same worn but immaculate appearance she had observed several weeks earlier, with the same commingling scents of perfumed soap and mustiness. She turned Jerome around to face a framed drawing: a skinny, bearded, naked man, parched tongue protruding, stood in a forest clearing next to a small round pond, his open hands catching the pond's submerged light. Stars formed crosses in the patch of sky above. Elegantly scribed below the stars were two lines:

Finally, at twilight, beneath old trees
The Deep Translucent Pond

Jerome pointed at the man. "Is that supposed to be him?" The words, *An old man singing* popped into his head. But this swollen-tongued man would be unable to sing.

"Maybe it's how he saw himself," Natalija replied.

"Old and starved?

"Thirsty. *Still* thirsty." She brought her hand close to the drawing's surface and spread her fingertips braille-like as she had so often seen the Black Magus do to commune with a writing.

"Why hang it in the bathroom?" Jerome asked. They surveyed the powder blue 1950s porcelain fixtures. Behind a floral-patterned shower curtain, dripping water plunked on the drain. Next to it, water shone placidly in a corner of the toilet bowl.

"Water" Jerome pronounced. "It's the room most closely associated with water." They glanced back and forth between the picture and the toilet bowl. It was a tight space and his nose grazed Natalija's hair. The silence and physical closeness became awkward and they edged toward the doorway. On the way out, Natalija reverently touched the picture frame.

They hovered uncertainly in the living room, careful to stay outside the three configured chairs as if cordoned off. "I wish he wasn't sitting like that," Jerome said, peering into the back room. "He looks too familiar. If he was laid out on the floor, I would know for sure he was gone."

Outside, a car braked in the gravel, followed by a slamming door then running steps. Tony plunged grey-faced through the front door. For once he wasn't wearing his Cleveland Indians hat, his long grey hair draped behind his ears. "Where?" They motioned at the back room. Tony strode across the room, Jerome and Natalija trailing. Halfway into the room Tony stopped. "I thought I told you not to let go!" he yelled. He came alongside the chair and knelt.

"I think it was his heart," Natalija said.

Tony looked into the Black Magus' face and patted his forearm. "It's okay, my friend. It's okay." Tony started speaking in a low voice, like a parent comforting a sullen child. Natalija and Jerome edged back into the living room.

After five minutes Tony came out, his eyes moist. "Did you call anyone?"

"Just you," Jerome said.

"We can stay," Natalija offered.

Tony stared at the floor. "I'll look after him."

"You need more time with him, don't you?" Natalija said.

Tony, stricken, gazed at the front door. "Once they take him through that door, I'll never see him again."

Natalija took him gently by the arm. "Let's find some kleenex." She led him toward the kitchen. Jerome gazed into the back room at the inert Black Magus. Sunlight through the window strengthened and under the chair he noticed a piece of paper. He re-entered the room, squatted behind the chair, reached under and retrieved a 4 x 6 index card. It was filled with writing in the Black Magus' hand, the lines small and difficult to read. Hearing Tony and Natalija approach he impulsively put the card in his shirt pocket.

Tony, holding Natalija's hand, led her into the room and took Jerome's hand "I want the two of you to do something. For *Him.*" His eyes, no longer moist, were stern. "I know baseball cards. Not poetry. Take the folders on the table. See that his work is finished." Jerome and Natalija nodded. Tony tightened his grip. "Do you swear to do this?"

Natalija clasped her other hand atop his. "We promise."

"Yes," Jerome added, "absolutely." Tony squeezed their hands and let go. Jerome and Natalija went over to the table and, starting at opposite ends, collected the folders, including the 11th.

Natalija turned to Tony. "There's one other thing. In the bathroom." Cradling folders in one arm, she went over to the chair and kissed the Black Magus' forehead. "Thank you," she wisped. She exited, wiping tears. Jerome, feeling he should do something similar, came alongside the chair. The Black Magus' face was paler, his teaching aura having further ebbed. Jerome opened his right hand in front of the slumping figure. "No calluses yet. But they're forming." He realized he had never touched the Black Magus, never shaken his hand or brushed fingers while exchanging writings. He rested his fingertips on the other man's large forearm, the skin deceptively warm from the sun. He was still unsure how to address him. "Thank you… Teacher." He sucked in his lips and turned away.

Tony and Natalija were waiting at the front door. Natalija held the framed picture from the bathroom. "For the cover of the 11th Book," she announced, as Jerome joined them.

"The 11th Book?"

"The writings in the 11th folder. His"

Jerome braced Tony's elbow. "Since his death was unexpected, the police need to be called. They'll want to talk to me. I'll circle back in an hour."

Tony tried to smile. "It'll be fine. It'll be fine."

Natalija and Jerome walked silently from the house. At their cars, she tried to hand him her share of the Triangulum folders. "You have more connections at the Literary League than I do."

Jerome refused her folders. "The base of the triangle is gone, but two sides remain."

She smiled bravely. He expected her to move away, but she stayed close, her herbal-scented hair commingling with the smell of sunlight on dying leaves. A lone yellow leaf drifted from above. They looked to see which tree it had fallen from, but all the branches were empty.

"What will you do for an hour?" Natalija asked.

Jerome gazed through bare trees at a soft blue sky. "Go to Headlands Beach. It's actually not bad for November."

Natalija turned to share his gaze. "Would you mind company?"

Headlands State Park looked abandoned. The leafless trees which divided the empty parking lots looked like burnt utility poles. The low scrubby dunes blocking the lake gave the illusion of an immense cliff-edge. Jerome pulled into the P-6 lot, littered with leaves, and Natalija pulled next to him.

"Not bad for November," Jerome said, realizing he was repeating himself. Natalija, wearing blue jeans, a long white sweater and wind breaker, gazed past the low dunes toward the lake, the faint breeze teasing her hair. Her green eyes, taking in the expanse, had a near and far timelessness and for a moment he wasn't sure who she was. He wished the Black Magus could see her now. He would know which Botticelli goddess.

They walked toward the break in the dunes to the six-trunked basswood where they had witnessed the water spout. Entering the break, the beach opened up, extending several hundred feet to the water's edge. They breathed in the damp smell of sand and decaying leaves, and the vast lake. The moss-stained picnic table was still in the same place.

"Do you want to walk, or sit?" Jerome asked. Natalija looked sadly at the table, then brightened. "The table! Our table." They sat on the same bench as before, facing outward toward the lake, and watched small waves rhythmically swish ashore. Out over the lake a slow moving herd of small white clouds migrated west to east.

"Have you ever seen a cloud move?" Natalija absently asked.

Jerome thought of the pencil drawing of himself lying in his sleeping bag, staring up into tree branches. Had the Black Magus guessed it actually happened? "Damn—I forgot!" He reached into his shirt pocket and pulled out the blue index card. "I found this under his chair." He held it between them. Natalija shifted closer and steadied one edge of the card between slender fingers. In full daylight the hastily scrawled lines were easier to read.

Morning Mythology

Standing waist deep in ground mist
As if I just waded into a lake

Watching the sun crest
My right hand twitches for something
A sword–
A broad sword I can raise
To catch the first flash
of molten light

Why this urge to be a swordsman
silhouetted against the sunrise?
Can a hand have ancient memories?

The next moment
an even older twinge:
My lower body concealed in mist
I could be a Centaur

Holding my sword high
I start to canter

Natalija ran a finger down the right margin. "Do you think he wrote it today?"

"There was a pencil on the floor. He probably dropped it along with the card when… it happened."

Natalija spread her tapered fingers braille-like over the card. "He kept his promise."

A tear ebbed down her cheek. She stopped breathing, then suddenly looped her near arm through his and pressed her head onto his chest. With her other hand she gripped his hand, which still held the card. Strands of her red-blonde hair blew across his neck.

Jerome gazed at the infinite water and sky. Gulls near and far flashed in shafts of sunlight. He wasn't sure if she was clinging to him, or to the past three months. Or to life. It didn't matter. The November sun warmed his face and a distant breeze caressed his forehead. *I have never known this.* He closed his eyes and felt the wind, the water, and the light. And her against him.

Acknowledgements

Special thanks to Linda Durnbaugh—writer, tutor to thousands, sojourner of the soul—for her keen editorial eye.

Infinite metaphysical indebtedness to The Magi in my life: Gerald Meluch and, in memorium, Doug Gardner (Tige).

About the Author

James Shelley, always an Ohioan, received history degrees from Miami University and Case Western which led to his first professional position as an archivist for the Rockefellers. Since then, he has been an adminstrator and taught humanities at the college level. Concerned about why so many young men in college falter, he founded an innovative advising program at Lakeland Community College to support at-risk male students, including ex-felons and minorities. His work on college men's issues has led to numerous interviews and articles in national media, including *The Atlantic and National Public Radio*.

Always he has written. Early playwriting led to performances of experimental works at Cleveland Public Theatre. His first published short story, *The Lion's Den*, earned an Ohio Arts Prize. As a poet, and in his writings on visual art, he promulgates for art which *gives* rather than *takes*. In his first novel, *The Deep Translucent Pond*, the main characters' poems provide "wormhole" interior glimpses, nudging the characters—usually while reaching for one another—towards magical moments of being.

Shelley resides in Chagrin Falls where he is honored to live with Mary Shelley. Communal interests include playing the bagpipes and appreciating the strange spectrum of human experiences it often presents: playing at a wedding one day, at a funeral the next.

Made in the USA
Coppell, TX
15 March 2022

75016124R00114